Frightful Friday

A Tabitha Chase Days of the Week Mystery
(Book 3)

Denise Jaden

Frightful Friday

A Tabitha Chase Days of the Week Mystery (Book 3)

By Denise Jaden

Tabby is finally ready to go on a casual date with Detective Jay Jameson at the local church's Harvest Festival, but her witch friends are holding their Fright Night fundraiser that same night. She feels caught in the middle of a long-standing quarrel between the two groups, especially when a dead body shows up at the center of it all.

As blame-shifting grows, will Tabby be able to figure out who is responsible for the corpse while keeping all of her friendships intact?

Join my mystery readers' newsletter today!

Sign up now, and you'll get access to a special mystery to accompany this series—an exclusive bonus for newsletter subscribers. In addition, you'll be the first to hear about new releases and receive special excerpts and behind-the-scenes bonuses.
Visit the link below to sign up and receive your bonus mystery:

https://www.subscribepage.com/mysterysignup

Chapter One

I HAD NO IDEA if I was dressed right for my first date with Detective Jay Jameson. I felt under-costumed for the typical Halloween parties I was used to attending back in Portland and over-dressed for a church's Harvest Festival. I'd been looking for hints for the past week—such as when Jay had taken his nephew shopping for overalls and when this red and white gingham dress mysteriously showed up in my aunt's bedroom closet. It wasn't the first time I experienced magical *happenings* aboard my late aunt's houseboat. They were slowly making me into a believer in the supernatural.

I spun in front of my full-length mirror, taking in my braided red pigtails and the extra-dark freckles I'd painted onto my cheeks for the night, wondering for the fiftieth time if it was too little or too much.

But I'd always been a fan of Halloween and of dressing up, and besides, I had an actual Halloween Fright Night party to go to after the church's Harvest Festival, so I was hoping this getup would serve both purposes.

After locking up the houseboat, I drove my own car to the outskirts of town where Crystal Cove Community Church had taken over one of the local farms to hold their harvest celebration.

I pulled into the gravel lot and navigated around the odd-angled parked cars. Country people parked differently than city people, I'd noticed since moving to Crystal Cove. Locals in this small town parked like they had all the room in the world, which I supposed they did. I wound around until I found Jay's dark sedan. Seeing his car gave me another pang of doubt. I was here to meet a police detective, for goodness sake. Why on earth had I thought it appropriate to dress like Holly Hobbie?

I took a deep breath and then stepped out of my car. My cat Sherlock had desperately wanted to join me tonight, but since I'd had no idea what kind of farm animals we might run into out at this location, I had decided it was better to attend animal-free. However, when I went to shut my car door, Sherlock popped his front paws up against my driver's seat from the back.

"You sneaky little tagalong." I pulled him up to look him in the eyes, a task made trickier by the spectacles he wore fastened around his head. Then I surveyed what I could see of the farm and didn't notice any roaming animals. I was secretly glad to not have to walk into the party alone. Lights were strung along a wall made of hay bales in the distance. Music streamed from that direction, too, so I had to assume that was where I'd find the Harvest Festival. Far in the distance was a large barn, hopefully keeping the farm animals in containment for the evening.

As I walked toward the music and lights, Sherlock let his stream-of-consciousness thoughts trickle into my mind, as though he wanted to get them all out now before we found the people.

Meeting Detective Jay? Must be an investigation. Danger! Suspects! Intrigue!

"No, nothing like that, buddy," I murmured. It was amazing how quickly I'd adapted to having these sorts of "conversations" with a cat. Before moving to Crystal Cove, I'd had my mind firmly rooted in reality, but since then,

I'd been learning to recognize strong emotion in my cat's inner voice. I knew he was already invested in these thoughts. "The only *danger* I expect tonight is if Jay tries to kiss me," I added.

My cheeks warmed, even though there was little chance of much romance happening between us, at least for tonight. Having his young nephew along would make sure of that. Tonight would be more friendship than anything else. With all the recent changes in my life, I'd made it clear I wasn't in a hurry to start dating anytime soon.

As I rounded the wall of hay bales, the surrounding area became immediately brighter with pot lights.

Hay bales ran in lines in four directions, creating a makeshift room, or perhaps more like a makeshift gymnasium, due to the large size. At least a hundred people of all ages laughed and talked and played carnival-type games around the perimeter—ring tosses and toy fishing and a lasso game. Country music played from the far end and there were three groups of four following the caller of a square dance. I was far from the only woman at this party wearing gingham. In fact, looking around, I would have almost guessed it was a requirement. In the center of the "room" I spotted Jay and his nephew, but as I moved closer, it seemed he was mid-argument with a couple of stout ladies in their seventies.

I didn't want to interrupt, and held back a few steps. The white-haired woman spoke so loudly she could be heard from a good distance away, even over the music.

"Don't you think you should be over there, shutting it down, rather than over here, partying the night away!" It sounded like a punctuated statement, more than a question.

"I'm afraid I'm off duty tonight, Mabel. And I'm here with Brady." He motioned to his nephew, whose face scrunched in worry at the tension.

"Well, somebody has to do something about them!" the other woman said. She looked a little younger, with her hair dyed a dark brown, but she had just as many wrinkles.

Jay bent down and said something quiet enough to Brady that I couldn't hear. The kid looked adorable in his oversized pair of denim overalls and painted freckles all over his cheeks that were much more obvious than mine. Jay pointed toward a fishing pond on the perimeter, but Brady clung to him. He couldn't have been more than five or six, awfully young to be on his own at this festival, even if it was put on by a local church.

Without taking time to rethink it, I swept forward and said, "I can take Brady fishing."

I wasn't sure if I was overstepping—I'd only met Brady once, after all. But Jay looked at me gratefully.

A second later, Brady squealed, and I had no idea why until he said, "Kitty!" and pointed up to my arms.

"Sure, let's go over here and pet the kitty," I told him, leading him away from the two angry women. As I bent and Brady asked my cat's name, I strained to hear more of the argument, while playing it casual for Brady.

Unfortunately, my cat was just as interested, and as soon as I placed him down in front of Brady, he strained back in Jay's direction.

"Sherlock," I said to both Brady and my cat. And then I took on a sternness to address only the cat. "Our job is to stay here. Nothing to worry about over there."

Sherlock hesitated, but then took a few steps back in our direction, thankfully keeping Brady's attention rapt, as it seemed Mabel and her friend were getting even more worked up.

Before I could finish that thought, Mabel grabbed her friend's arm and pulled her toward the gap in hay bales to the parking lot.

I stood as Jay approached. "What were they so upset about?" I asked.

Jay sighed. "The church members started this festival last year, to give locals an alternative to the dark and scary events put on by the witches. Your Aunt Lizzie used to be somewhat of a bridge between the two groups. She brought an awareness that the Crystal Cove witches didn't focus on dark magic, but were meant to be a force of good in this town. But since then, the church has brought on a new pastor who doesn't understand the nuances, and with Marigold Weathers often playing up the darker side of her magic, it seems there's a growing feud between the two groups again. It doesn't help that the witches have gone all out this year with their Fright Night haunted house. Many of the church members think the local police should shut it down for the safety and reputation of the town."

Jay rolled his eyes, but I felt slightly guilty, as I hadn't told him that the reason I'd wanted to bring my own vehicle tonight was because I planned to go and support the witches at their haunted house when I was done here. It was a fundraiser, in hopes that they'd be able to afford to put on their Winter Solstice Festival later this year. Even though I'd never celebrated the holiday myself, many of the witches were becoming my friends since moving to town, and I was quite certain there was nothing dark or evil about their powers. If this fundraiser was something they cared about, I wanted to support them.

"Did they go to try and shut it down themselves?" I asked, trying to picture Mabel and her friend going up against Marigold, Ruth, and the other able-bodied witches.

Jay shook his head. "I told them they should call their concerns into the station. In a small town, it's easy for people to think a detective is on duty all the time, and so our department has a policy, especially when it comes to non-emergencies. We re-direct people to whoever's on duty at the station, and that allows the others of us to get some actual time off."

I'd only known Jay a few months, but even I could think of several times that he'd been suddenly needed for a case, even though he wasn't officially on duty. I was glad to see him setting some boundaries with these church ladies.

Soon after, Jay and I moved along to the carnival games, taking in each one for as long as it held young Brady's attention. "Look, Uncle Jay! I won a bag of candy!"

"Great!" Jay said, putting his hand out for it. Brady obediently passed it over and Jay told me, "My sister and her husband aren't big on giving him sugar." I felt immediately sad for the kid, having his candy taken away from him on Halloween.

But then Brady told me, "If I don't eat any, Mommy will trade me for a toy tomorrow." He grinned brightly enough that I figured it was a fair trade.

Thankfully, Brady wasn't interested in square dancing, as I hadn't tried anything of the sort since eighth grade.

When a man in a cowboy hat announced that the next hayride was set to leave in five minutes, Jay got boyishly excited and insisted we do that next. I couldn't quite understand the thrill, but I didn't complain, since I was just as happy to avoid the dancing.

A tractor led a long trailer filled with hay bales along a path on the outskirts of the farm, lit only by the moon and twinkle lights. As the hay bales jostled us along the dirt path, my leg kept knocking against Jay's, and I couldn't help but think of how romantic this might have been if he didn't have his nephew on his lap and if I didn't have Sherlock on mine.

At the end of the ride, as we climbed off of the trailer at the entry way to the festival area, we saw the two angry women again, but thankfully this time their attention was not on Jay.

They had a young woman between them with wild red curly hair and bloodshot eyes.

"Come with us," Mabel told the distraught woman in a voice that had changed to pure compassion. "We'll get you into the festival and get your mind off of your poor lost brother."

But the lady seemed to have no interest in the celebrations. She seemed to be trying to pull the ladies away from the celebration. "No! I can't have fun! I came here to pray. I need some answers!"

Mabel and her friend gave each other a look over the crazed lady, who now bent forward to cry into her hands. "Why don't we help Carla find some of the elders," Mabel said to her friend, and then they led the lady around the perimeter of the hay bale walls. "We will pray and help you find some peace about your brother."

As they moved out of earshot, it looked as though Mabel's words weren't bringing the woman any peace so far.

Jay wore a smirk that he looked like he was suppressing.

"What?" I asked.

He shrugged. "Sometimes I think disgruntled people are only really looking for purpose. Now Mabel and Edith have some purpose—at least for the next little while."

I suspected Mabel and Edith weren't all too happy with the purpose they had been given for the evening, but I was just glad it had gotten them off of Jay's case.

Thankfully, we didn't see the two elderly ladies again, and even though two more people came up to Jay, wanting to discuss their displeasure with Fright Night, he cut them off, telling them that Mabel had already called in a complaint to the station.

It wasn't even eight-thirty when Brady let out a big yawn and stretched his arms above his head. Jay didn't fail to notice. "I'd better get this big guy home to get some sleep."

"So early?" Even though I asked this, I was glad. That way I wouldn't have to make up an excuse of why I, too, should be heading out to my other commitment.

Jay nodded as he picked Brady up, nuzzled him to his neck, and led the way toward the parking lot. "My sister's husband has strict rules about bedtime with him. Brady's used to falling asleep by nine, and he wouldn't be able to keep his eyes open much longer even if we stayed." After a beat, where he seemed to debate the words, he looked at me and said in a leading tone, "And you're off to…?"

I looked both directions. I knew Jay would understand, but perhaps others in the vicinity wouldn't. As we arrived at his car, we were alone, except for one man who sat a few cars down in his vehicle with his hands rubbing back and forth against his steering wheel. He was a big guy, looked like a bodybuilder type, but I wondered if he was having as much trouble working up the courage to walk into the Harvest Festival alone as I had. It was never fun to attend social functions alone.

I tried to give the man an understanding smile, but his eyes stayed straight ahead. Eventually, I turned back to Jay and dropped my voice. "I said I'd help Marigold and the others with their fundraiser." I hoped keeping the title of the event and the word "witches" out of it would help not to draw attention from any lurking ears.

Jay bent and slid Brady into the backseat, belting him in. If he was half-awake when Jay had opened the door, that last bit of wakefulness faded with the comfort of his booster seat. Jay wasn't kidding about the kid falling asleep like clockwork.

"You're up for scary things, then?" Jay asked as he stood. I wondered if he was fishing for an invitation. But, no. He had to watch Brady until his sister Brit got off work at ten.

"Me? No way. But they seemed like they were eager for help, and they've been great about welcoming me to town, so…"

"I only ask because I assume you haven't been to one of their 'fundraisers' before." He used air quotes. I couldn't tell if his voice was meant to frighten me or tease me.

I suddenly didn't feel like joking. "Wh-why?" My mouth went dry.

He smirked, and the teasing took over. I still wasn't sure I was ready to go there, though. Especially when he told me, "Their haunted houses aren't your typical fake creepy spiders, especially now that Marigold is in charge. That's all."

I nibbled my lip in nervousness, but Jay didn't seem to notice.

"I'd better get this one home to his own bed," he told me. "Have fun with your friends."

Again with the smirk. Again with the teasing tone.

But my stomach was clenched and my mouth was a desert as I watched him drive off and got into my car with Sherlock, wondering if I'd made an offer I might not be able to keep.

Chapter Two

I stopped by The Heirloom Café on my way across town. Even though Olivia had been great about giving me the night off from serving coffee and other hot drinks, I felt like I needed a chamomile tea to take along to help settle my nerves.

When I walked through the café's front door, the place was quieter than I'd ever seen it. Not a single customer, and Olivia, who never seemed to slow down, was sitting at a table, reading a book.

She perked up and put her book down, though, the moment she heard the door chime.

"It's okay," I told her. "Stay where you are. I stopped by to grab a cup of tea, but I can make it myself."

Olivia hesitated, but then put her feet back up on a nearby chair. It was nice to see her relaxing a little. "Don't you look cute? I thought you were super busy with two big events tonight?" she asked.

I sighed. "I was. I mean, I am. I'm in between them right now. Jay had to get his nephew home to bed. Has it been this dead all night?"

Olivia nodded. "We get a few kids trick-or-treating early on, but then it's always a ghost town on Halloween after that. Everyone in town either wants to be at the harvest festival or Fright Night." She gave a wry smile. "It's my first time missing the haunted house in years."

I stopped pouring the hot water over my tea bag. "Wait, you wanted to go? Why didn't you tell me?"

She waved a casual hand. "You were excited for your date. I'm sad to see it didn't last very long."

It had been pretty perfect, despite the short length. I had a sudden idea. "Hey, why don't I watch the café for half an hour so you can go take a quick walk through the haunted house?" It was the least I could do, when tonight was supposed to be my shift.

She kicked her feet down from the chair. "Are you sure?" She was already standing, her face alight with sudden energy.

"Of course." Yes, maybe I was only stalling about going there myself. But I hoped sitting alone in an empty coffee shop would help calm my nerves a little before going to face the scariness. "Let me grab Sherlock from my car first."

Sherlock wasn't happy at all with me when I told him we weren't going to Fright Night quite yet. In fact, he was so unhappy, he stubbornly lay down on the passenger seat and gripped at the velour when I tried to pick him up.

"Fine, you want to wait here?"

I left him behind, but felt lonely as Olivia left and I was all alone in the café. To pass the time, I cleaned the already clean café, and thought again about my first date with Jay.

He'd been great about keeping it low pressure. It made me think I was ready to go out for dinner with him, or on an actual one-on-one date, without his nephew chaperoning.

Nine-thirty passed, and it was almost ten before Olivia finally arrived back at the café, barely in time to close up. Her ease from when I'd first seen her this evening had completely evaporated as she whisked through the café door.

"So sorry I took so long!" she said. "The power went out right in the middle of my trek through the haunted house. I have to admit, it's the first time I've been really rattled by one of their Fright Nights."

She looked rattled, with her hair coming loose from her dark ponytail, and her hands rubbing together, like they were sweaty.

Now I really didn't want to go there. I'd already thrown out my paper cup, but I eyed the chamomile tea container on the shelf. "Did they get the power back on?"

She chuckled. "Oh, yes. It was only off for about five minutes, but during those five minutes, witches all around chanted in scary voices, 'Stay right where you are!' and 'Don't move a muscle!'"

I looked up at the ceiling, wanting to leave even less.

"It was probably only part of their shtick. It certainly worked to rattle all of us who were in there. Hey, you'd better get over there before they shut it down for the night."

I sighed inwardly. "Yeah, I guess I'd better."

I hadn't even driven all the way down Fifth Street when my palms broke into a wild sweat against the steering wheel. The trees lining the road were webbed with some sort of creepy netting, as though from giant spiders. What I hoped were fabric ghosts, more gray and translucent than white, caught the light of the moon from behind the trees every few feet and fluttered eerily in the light breeze.

I was still learning about the local magic. The only magic I'd experienced included strong impressions, cute clothing showing up in my closet, and a talking cat. Even though I didn't think the witches of Crystal Cove took part in any evil sort of magic, they did take their practices very seriously. I'd only ever seen the witches use magic for good, and in small ways, but I didn't know for a fact that none of them were attempting to channel darker powers or tamper in things better left untouched. Who was to say that my witch friends wouldn't be able to conjure up actual ghosts?

This area wasn't as thickly populated as areas closer to the town center. Houses were spaced out and even though people in costumes moved along the street, they were so sporadic that they didn't provide any real sense of safety. Out of my peripheral vision, I also saw people sitting in their cars parked on the side of the road, probably trying to work up the courage to go in.

It's a haunted house, Tabby, I told myself for the twentieth time. *Calm down.*

In costumes, I couldn't tell the difference between teenagers and adults. I also couldn't recognize anyone from town I might know.

Ever since Olivia had given me the evening barista shift at The Heirloom Café, I'd been priding myself on meeting lots of locals, but the realization that I may not be able to recognize a single one of them left me feeling lonely already.

The mansion the witches had rented to hold their Fright Night haunted house was at the end of the block and soon came into view. I found a spot along the curb and parked. Sherlock let out a loud meow, making me jump. I'd completely forgotten he was with me, as he'd been silently pouting the entire drive here.

"Even with you along, I don't think I can do it," I told him, while staring ahead at the giant creepy house, spider webbing evident from even fifty feet away. "I'll give a donation tomorrow. That will have to be enough."

But Sherlock meowed again, letting me know what he thought of my cowardly attitude.

"Fine." I rolled my eyes and reached for my door handle with one hand and Sherlock with the other, before I could change my mind. Sherlock squirmed in my arms, and even though I suspected his reaction was more about wanting to get down and explore than being afraid, I told him, "Oh, you'd better believe you're coming with me."

Thankfully, before we made it within a hundred feet of the mansion, familiarity caught my eye. Under a wooden booth with a sign that read TICKETS stood Marigold Weathers, the queen bee of all the local witches, all decked out in her usual purple poufy hair and ground-length shimmery orange dress.

"I'm sorry I'm so late," I called as I picked up my pace toward her. I let Sherlock down when I was a few feet away, as Marigold wasn't much of a cat person. She had just handed a costumed couple two tickets and what looked like a skull-shaped flashlight. They scampered off toward the entry of the mansion with excited grins.

Marigold looked me up and down with a raised eyebrow and I pulled my coat closed over my gingham dress. Thankfully, she didn't comment, as I didn't want to mention I'd been at the church's Harvest Festival, as the tension there could go both ways.

"How has it been going?"

"Fine. At least now it is." Marigold harrumphed and picked at her hair and her dress as though even her clothes were annoying her. "The power went out not long ago, though, and I'd bet my life that those church ladies were behind it. First they get the mayor to slap us with a curfew, and then they cut our power?"

So the power outage wasn't part of their shtick. The tension definitely went both ways. "Yes, I heard. But it looks like you have power now," I observed, trying to get her off of her rant before it got too heated.

She sighed. "Yes. Someone flipped the main breaker at the electrical meter, probably figuring we wouldn't know how to find it and flip it back on." She shook her head, speaking as though I might challenge her on this. "It was definitely deliberate."

I couldn't envision Marigold even knowing where to find the electrical meter, let alone flipping on or off a main breaker. Even less could I picture Mabel and Edith knowing about those things.

Thankfully, Marigold switched topics. "Most of the locals have been through the haunted house at least twice. One lady went through five times!" She let out a hearty laugh. "Now we're just expecting the stragglers who got off work late."

I wondered what kind of a haunted house warranted not one terrifying traipse through its scary halls but *five*. I looked toward the open doors again, dark and creepy inside. I couldn't see anything else.

"Are you ready—" Marigold started, but I cut her off, not wanting to have to make up an excuse for how scared I was.

"I'm sure you're ready for a break, what with having to deal with the power problem and everything. Why don't you show me what to do and I'll take over ticket sales so you can make sure everything's running smoothly inside?"

"Are you sure?" She always wanted to be everywhere at once, so she was quick to take me up on my offer.

I moved around the tickets sign and reached for the cash box, but she yanked it back toward her chest when my hand had barely touched it. "Oh?" I asked as a question. I couldn't very well take over ticket sales without any money to make change for patrons.

She seemed to realize this and plunked the metal box back onto the small wooden shelf in front of her. But then she turned, as if shielding it from me with her body as she opened it.

It seemed so strange, but because she couldn't completely block my view, I saw past her shoulder to stacks of not only twenties, but hundred dollar bills within the box.

My eyes widened. There had to be several thousand dollars in there! I didn't quite know what to ask as she turned back around and passed me a much smaller stack of fives and tens.

"Most of the locals have already been through, so you shouldn't need much," she explained, re-locking the box and gripping its handle firmly.

In truth, I didn't want to be responsible for that hefty amount of money, and yet, something about her protectiveness of it—from me—made me feel like an outsider in this town all over again.

Without an ounce of worry about how she may or may not have offended me, Marigold strode off toward the haunted mansion with her own skull flashlight and her ground-length shimmery orange dress flowing behind her. She was correct about the attendance slowing down. In the next hour, I only sold five more tickets at the surprisingly high price of twenty dollars each. But no one seemed bothered by paying it.

I had considered giving my own twenty-dollar donation, since I felt badly about not wanting to actually take part in their fundraiser, but now I felt a little cheap if that was all I gave. Still, working at The Heirloom Café in the evenings didn't leave me with a lot of extra cash, and the houseboat rental season slowed down dramatically after the end of summer, so I wasn't bringing in anything from that at the moment.

I looked toward the front entrance again and snuggled deeper into my coat, still feeling a little too peppy, not to mention cold, in my gingham dress. My chill only came partly from the night air, though. The other part was definitely from what might lay inside the mansion. As the thrill-loving stragglers dissipated and I was left outside on my own, my mind played tricks on me and I started to see movement in every nearby tree or bush.

"Sherlock?" I had to keep calling him over. He was creeping around exploring, and it made me feel slightly better to have him in my sight.

My parents had always told me I had an overactive imagination. It was true. I'd never been able to watch movies with even the slightest bit of suspense or my mind would go crazy and I'd end up shrieking at the smallest creak of a floor. Aunt Lizzie was the only person I'd ever known who had treated my overactive imagination as a good thing—as though I could simply see more in this world than most. I missed her terribly, especially tonight, when she'd know what to say to me to both calm me down and give me a sense of peace about the unique person I was.

A couple strolled my way in matching skeleton costumes. These ones weren't too scary—with painted bones on black clothes and their faces wearing only a hint of black and white makeup.

"Two tickets to Fright Night?" I guessed.

The woman nodded and passed over two twenties. Under the makeup, I would have guessed her to be my age. I angled my head, trying to see past their costumes for familiarity.

"It's the one night of the year we can get into the Kelsey mansion," the man said, looking eager to head toward the front doors before I'd even given them their flashlight. "See what updates he's done. Gotta take advantage of that."

"The owner of the mansion does regular remodels?" I asked, my realtor brain perking up automatically at the suggestion.

The woman nodded. "Last year, he added a billiard room. Of course it was a little hard to see beyond the spider webs and carcasses…" She laughed while I let out a shiver.

"Are you folks from Crystal Cove?" I hadn't found familiarity in their faces, but I didn't particularly want them to leave me alone out here, at least not so quickly.

The man had already moved a few feet away to examine the brick posts lining the mansion's driveway, so the woman answered. "No, we're from Eugene. My husband's a realtor, specializing in larger properties. He's been trying to talk Matthew Kelsey into selling this place for ages. Each year we drive in to see what he's done with the place and Donny—" She motioned to the other skeleton, "he writes up a whole property improvement and assessment report." The woman sighed, as though this was a long-term frustration. "Donny's always hated the word no, and so he treats it as his personal challenge to get Mr. Kelsey to finally list with him."

The name Kelsey sounded familiar to me, but I figured I'd probably heard Marigold or one of the other witches mention it while planning their haunted house.

The woman thanked me for the tickets and flashlight and caught up to her husband before I could ask her name. But I locked the name Donny, the realtor from Eugene, into my mind. I could always ask Marigold if she knew him later.

Sherlock rubbed up against my calves, making me almost come out of my skin.

Excitement inside? He asked what sounded like a simple question, but the words made me feel even more cowardly.

Instead, I focused on the part that intrigued me more than scared me. "I am interested in what kind of improvements have been done to the mansion. Maybe if we stick around to help clean up, we can see it?" I added the words, *with the lights on*, only in my head.

It was another fifteen minutes before I saw another witch, and this time it was my friend Rachael who appeared.

"Are you still getting any customers?" Rachael looked especially witchy tonight, wearing not only her usual short black skirt and black-and-white striped tights, but also a pointed witch's hat, which had apparently been passed down from her grandmother.

I shook my head. "The last ones were probably fifteen minutes ago."

She nodded, looking unsurprised, and then flipped a wooden sign on the front of the booth from OPEN to CLOSED. "Thanks for your help, Tabby. I'll let the others know we can start packing up. I thought we had until midnight, but now Marigold's saying 11:45."

That wasn't much more than half an hour from now. I pulled the money out of my pocket from where I'd been stashing twenties. "What should I do with this?"

She twisted her lips. "Can you keep it until tomorrow?"

It was just like Rachael to be so easily trusting, but I wondered if Marigold would hold the same sentiments. "Actually, can you take it?"

She looked at me with a cocked eyebrow, but at least she took it from my hand.

Rather than explaining, I changed the subject. "I don't have to work until tomorrow afternoon. I thought I might stay and help with the cleanup." It was the least I could do, since I couldn't find it in me to *enjoy* the fruits of their labor, and besides, with the mayor's enforced curfew, they didn't have a lot of time to pack up all the décor.

Her eyes lit up at my offer. "Oh, that'd be great! Marigold's in such a panic to get everything cleaned up on time. I don't know why it's such a big deal, since usually Mr. Kelsey lets us finish cleaning up the day after Halloween, but I guess he must want us out early this year for some reason. I'll get the main lights on. Do you want to carry some of those bins inside, so we can load them up?" She motioned to a stack of empty orange extra-large packing bins, each big enough to fit a half-dozen full-size jack-o-lanterns.

With that in mind, I started with the jack-o-lanterns lining the path. Even though they looked real from a distance, carved with ghoulish faces, and lit by flickering candles, as I moved close to the first one and picked it up, I realized the whole thing was plastic, even the fake flickering candle. It weighed less than a pound of butter.

My stalling and deconstructing of the outside of the mansion worked out well, because by the time I filled the first two bins and had taken down everything that wouldn't require a ladder, the lights in the mansion illuminated the windows and three witches streamed out the front entrance, arms filled with what looked like full-grown zombies.

I reminded myself of how real the jack-o-lanterns had looked, and how fake they were in reality. Each witch carried at least three zombies, so they had to be just as fake.

I forced a deep breath, trying to relax, and marched toward the front door, where Marigold stood, calling out directions.

"I'm here to help," I told her.

With the lights on, Marigold showed her sixty-three years, with wrinkles around her eyes and grey edges around the roots of her purple hair. "Take those bins down to the witches in the basement so they can start cleaning up there."

While I didn't love the sound of "basement," I was at least comforted by the fact that I'd find other witches around to help me. Hopefully, one would be Rachael.

Sherlock attempted to follow me inside and into a hallway that was double the width of any hallway I'd ever seen—even in my parents' oversized house.

"The cat stays outside." Marigold eyed my cat and shook her head. "Can you imagine?" she asked more to herself than to me.

She quickly moved back outside, calling out packing orders to others as she went. I gave Sherlock a little backhanded wave, but he'd heard Marigold's instruction and was already strutting down the front steps. He skittered off into the bushes, probably so he wouldn't catch anymore of her disgruntled attitude.

As I walked down the hall, my eyes were drawn past the spider webs draped all around, and instead found the architecture beneath. The Georgian crown moulding lined the length of the hallway and the pilasters around the doorways had a rich Roman feel. Suddenly, I could understand the skeleton couple's interest in driving all the way from Eugene to see this place every year.

I peeked into each open doorway, even though many of them were roped off with crime-scene tape. I quickly found the billiard room Donny had traveled to see last year, and indeed, the mouldings in that room appeared more modern, while still matching the golden tones of those in the hallway.

I figured now that the haunted house decorations all had to come down, it couldn't hurt to pull at the crime-scene tape so I could poke my head in for a closer look. There were a few zombie bodies spread out around the room. One was splayed across the pool table; another had the curtain rope strung around its neck and hung right inside the window. I'd seen its shape from out at my station in the ticket booth earlier, and it had been one of the first things to give me the creeps about this place.

But seeing it now, in the light, gave me a bit of peace. I could picture the witches throwing all the zombies in this room over their arms and heading outside with them like they weighed about as much as a balloon.

The least I could do was pack a few of them into a bin, if I was so determined to take an extra minute to appreciate the architecture.

I had to hold my breath as I unwrapped the zombie from the curtain rope, but within minutes I had the entire billiard room cleaned up and I could see it for the well-appointed room it was. This Matthew Kelsey had good taste. I wondered if this was his year-round home, and if so, where he was tonight.

As that thought occurred to me, I figured out where I knew the name from. Wasn't a man named Kelsey running for mayor in the upcoming election? If he won, I wondered if he'd be stricter or less strict with things like curfews for the witches' activities.

I had finished cleaning out the next room—a smaller sitting room—before I admitted to myself that what I was really doing was stalling from descending into the basement.

That became even more apparent when two witches hefting garbage bags passed me down the hall. The one I knew, Ruth, muttered something about the amount of mess the patrons had left as she passed. "If they can't hold their stomachs, they shouldn't be wandering through a haunted house, now should they?"

I looked again at the crime scene tape cordoning off the next room and made a split-second decision. Clearly, these upper rooms were only for gazing at from far away. The zombies and spider webs certainly looked real—but only from a distance. As I moved closer to each one, and especially when I picked them up, all the décor quickly became fabrications.

Ruth and her witch-friend headed back inside from dropping off their trash, and as they passed me, Ruth said, "Oh, thanks so much for cleaning the upstairs, Tabby."

I smiled and pointed past the stairwell, to the next room, which now that I thought about it, probably had had even less foot traffic. "I'm slipping the decorations from this floor into the orange bins. That's okay?" I mentally crossed all of my fingers and toes until she nodded.

"I think some of the windows in the upper floors also have hanging bodies, if you want to grab those next?"

I let out a shiver at the words "hanging bodies," but quickly agreed and passed along some of my empty bins to her so she could take them to the basement. It seemed I had landed one of the least scary and grotesque jobs in this cleanup, and I couldn't be happier. As they moved out of view, I hauled the rest of my empty bins past the stairwell and to the next room, which turned out to be a bathroom. It was also well appointed, with brass faucets and a claw-foot tub that at any other time I would have guessed went completely unused, but the witches had really gone all out tonight.

Not only was one of their zombie bodies in the tub, but they'd filled it with dry ice, which let off a nice amount of steam around the fake carcass.

As I moved closer, an odd smell hit my nose, like pickles or vinegar. I looked around the base of the tub, wondering if there might be some sort of a fan pumping out the dry ice, bit it didn't appear to be plugged in anywhere. It looked as though the zombie was just plunked down on a bed of dry ice so thick that I could only clearly make out its head. It appeared to be surrounded by stalks of dried rosemary. I wondered if the zombie would be soaking wet, and if I'd have to find a way of drying it out before packing it away in a sealable bin.

I grasped the shoulder of it to pick it up and examine it, but then I froze in place. This zombie felt different. Very different. Not like the beige fabric construction of the others I'd pulled down. There was some weight to it that didn't feel like water—I could tell this without even trying to move it. The eyes looked sunken, like many of the other zombies, but this one took realism to a whole new level. The glassy eyes stared up at me as though they had seen a world of events before making it into this tub.

Staring into its vacant eyes, I snatched my hand away before I even realized why.

Then my mouth opened and I let out a loud shriek.

Because this wasn't a zombie decoration at all.

This was a real body.

Chapter Three

RACHAEL WAS THE FIRST witch to arrive at my side. I had taken a couple of steps away from the tub, but I couldn't take my eyes off of the body as I asked her, "Is that…is that one of your decorations?"

The question sounded ridiculous to my own ears—what would the witches be doing with a real corpse?—but I couldn't help hoping I had made a mistake even as my instincts told me I hadn't.

She took a step toward the tub, but my arm, on reflex, darted out to hold her back.

"We probably shouldn't touch it." Unfortunately, since arriving in Crystal Cove, I'd been privy to two dead bodies. Those two instances had been enough to drill into my mind that dead bodies should not be touched.

She pulled her hat off and bent down, studying the body and the tub from different angles, but still at a distance. "I don't think so. And Marigold told us not to bother decorating this end of the hallway, since no one would be coming down this way."

I squinted. "But the dry ice and everything. It seems like someone went to a lot of trouble..."

"You know, Marigold was freaking out earlier, right after the power came back on, because there wasn't enough dry ice to fill the machines in the basement. Ruth had to call CJ at home and beg him to meet her at Happy Hardware to get more."

CJ was the owner of our local hardware store, a nice man in his sixties. He'd told me more than once since I'd moved to Crystal Cove that people tended to blame their problems on the local hardware store owner. I hoped Ruth hadn't done that. Or worse, Marigold.

"So maybe Ruth got too much and they disposed of the extra in this tub?"

Rachael nodded slowly. "I guess so."

I pulled out my phone, and without thinking twice, dialed Jay. I expected he'd have been home a long time ago, and might even be in bed by now, but he answered on the first ring, as if on high alert.

"Can I call you back, Tabby?" he asked, by way of a hello.

"Well, um, no." As usual, I hadn't thought about how to explain myself until I was already in the midst of doing so. "I'm at the Fright Night haunted house, and, well, something's happened here."

Background noise came through the phone. Cars and serious voices. He either wasn't at home or he had his TV on really loud.

Then a siren sounded, and another thought occurred to me. "Wait, are you at a crime scene?"

"Yeah, I got called back out to the Harvest Festival. A woman was hit by a car. Can I call you back?" he asked again.

I stared at the vacant eyes of the body I'd just discovered and willed myself to believe it was only a decoration. But at the same time, I couldn't bring myself to move closer to find proof. "I think we have a situation over here, too," I said. "But I can call the station."

"Probably a good idea," Jay said. "I'll get over there as soon as I can, but I could still be a while."

I told him not to worry and hung up. Rather than calling the station directly, I called the other local detective I had on speed dial: Aaron Thom.

As the phone rang, I cupped the mouthpiece and whispered to Rachael, "Why don't you go tell Marigold what we discovered?"

Rachael hesitated and her forehead creased. "But…she's in such a hurry to pack up." Rachael's excuse must have sounded weak to her own ears as well, because a second later, she dipped her head and left. I took in a deep breath and almost choked on the strong scent. I hated being left in this small room with what I was now convinced was a body that had been dead for more than a few hours. I suspected what I smelled was not pickle juice, but rather formaldehyde.

Aaron sounded equally in the middle of business when he answered, but then again, that was how he always sounded.

"What do you need, Tabitha?" he asked.

I explained to him where I was and what I'd found, but I had barely strung together a couple of sentences when he cut me off.

"Hang on. You? You discovered *another* dead body?"

I swallowed hard, knowing how this must look. But at least when I'd come face to face with the last dead body, Jay had been with me. That had to mean something, although I wasn't sure quite what.

"I was only here to help them pack up." If I had to, I'd explain that the only reason I had been the one to discover this particular body was because I was too much of a chicken to have descended into the bowels of this haunted extravaganza. "It looks a lot like the other decorations and it was only when I went to pack it up that I realized it wasn't made of flimsy fabric like the others."

"You didn't move it, did you?" His accusatory tone brought me back to the first night I'd met him on the roadside. But I'd learned since then that he spoke that way to everyone, and it was one of the qualities that made him great at his job.

"I didn't. I swear. As soon as I realized he was real, I backed away and haven't touched a thing."

"Good, good," he told me. "Keep every one else away, too, and I'll be there as soon as I can."

Chapter Four

I sat against the wall across from the bathroom, guarding the door from anyone entering, and tried to gulp in some deep breaths of fresh air while I waited for Aaron to arrive. I could still smell the formaldehyde as though it now permanently lined my nostrils.

Soon, my forced calmness was interrupted when Marigold stormed down the wide hallway toward me with three witches, including Rachael, in her wake. Marigold's forehead contorted in anger and she didn't seem to notice me sitting here. Her gaze was planted squarely on the bathroom door across from me as she murmured something that sounded like "It's almost time and we're nowhere near cleaned up yet."

I sprang to my feet.

"Stop! Detective Thom is on his way!" I practically shouted, in order to stop her in her tracks.

"No!" Her eyes widened toward Rachael. She slowed but didn't stop. "Shhh!" she hissed at me. "Do you want everyone to hear?" Her gaze darted around, even though the hallway was deserted. "Besides, you don't know what you're talking about. It's only one of our better decorations." Marigold turned and spoke to the witches behind her. "See, I told you that outsiders only cause more problems."

I opened my mouth, but nothing came out. Was she seriously blaming this on me? Finally, I coaxed out some words. "This was no decoration, Marigold. Trust me. I touched it." I could still sense the supple and velvety wrinkles of the body's skin against my fingertips.

"Oh, you're allowed to go in and play around with it, and we're not?" Marigold's bright purple hair made her face appear extra red when she was angry—which seemed to be a regular occurrence.

"Believe me, I wasn't *playing* with it!" My indignation rose, and I moved closer to the bathroom door, as if I might be able to block them all from going inside. "Like I said, Detective Thom is on his way. You need to wait and talk to him before going anywhere near this room. Besides, Rachael said this area of the mansion wasn't even decorated."

Rachael's gaze immediately fell to her striped tights, and I felt bad for throwing her into the blame, but Marigold wasn't listening to reason, and I wasn't about to get blamed for another murder scene being tampered with if I could help it.

"It wasn't supposed to be," Marigold gritted out. "But you know some of these younger witches. They go crazy with this sort of thing. They want to make it as real as possible."

She was still trying to convince herself I had only mistaken one of their decorations for a dead body. "I don't see what waiting for Detective Thom will hurt," I murmured more quietly, having some compassion for her misunderstanding. I wouldn't have wanted to believe it either in her place.

But she huffed out a laugh at me. "What will it hurt? As soon as the police get involved, the story will run through the town like wildfire." She huffed again. "Oh, wait. I forgot. You're not from Crystal Cove. You wouldn't understand."

I pulled back, feeling as though I'd been slapped. I'd thought Marigold and I were becoming friends. But I reminded myself of her polarizing personality. She was lovely if she thought you were on her side about whatever particular cause she'd taken up. But she could turn on a dime.

And the thing was, she wasn't wrong about local gossip. It *did* spread like wildfire. I'd overheard more than my share of the local gossip during my shifts at The Heirloom Café.

I spoke the argument that kept niggling away at me. "This is a haunted house, though. Don't you think a little gossip about a real dead body being discovered would make it even more popular, not less?" This may not be true with the regular churchgoers of Crystal Cove, but it should be true of those looking for a scary haunted house.

Marigold opened her mouth, but nothing immediately came out. For the first time since I had met her, Marigold didn't have an argument right on the tip of her tongue. She clearly hadn't thought of this, and her pause to ponder my suggestion was long enough that it gave Aaron time to arrive.

I pointed down the hall toward the front doors, which had been propped open. "Look, the police are here now!" Red and blue lights emanated from the street, even though Aaron's car was out of view.

Marigold huffed again, but she pulled her witch-friends back toward the billiard room, murmuring, "Come on. Let's discuss how to get ahead of this story before it's all over town."

Rachael looked over her shoulder at me as she followed Marigold down the hall. She didn't look like she hated me at least. She had been there, after all, and seen my stark reaction to the body.

But as she followed them into the billiard room, I was reminded once again that magic was most often thicker than friendship in this town.

Seconds later, Aaron stormed down the hallway toward me with Mick, the local medical examiner on his heels.

I had the sudden sickening thought: what if Marigold was right? What if I'd only mistaken an elaborate decoration for a dead body? I had been the only person to have a close look at it, after all.

"Who's in charge of this event?" Aaron barked at me, when he was still twenty feet away.

"Um. Marigold Weathers?" I asked it as a question, in little more than a whisper. I certainly didn't want it to sound as though I was accusing her of anything—not while she was within ear shot. I motioned to the billiard room as he passed, but he ignored my hand gestures and walked straight for the bathroom across from me, as though he had a sixth sense for where to find dead bodies.

"It's in here." I'm sure it was supposed to be a question, but as usual, with Aaron's natural authority, it came out as a proclamation.

"Yes," I eked out, more to Mick than to Aaron, as the detective had already disappeared into the small room.

Mick and I had never been formally introduced, but as Crystal Cove was such a small town, he had always been on the scene at local tragedies of this kind. So this was my third time seeing his serious expression.

I had once asked Jay if it was strange, how many murders Crystal Cove seemed to experience, after the last time I'd helped solve one. He'd gone on to explain that murders, or even simply unexplained deaths, were more common in coastal towns, with so many transient tourists. Even so, he said that the number of murders that occurred in Crystal

Cove was higher than most coastal towns, an unexplained mystery even to the police. It had made me rethink living here, but only for a moment. I had made too many friends, and felt like I fit in here like I'd never fit in anywhere before. At least I'd thought so before I'd seen Marigold turn on me tonight. What if she turned the rest of her witch friends against me?

Then again, what if Jay was right and I actually had a bit of a knack for helping to solve these sorts of mysteries?

What I'd neglected asking—maybe because I didn't want to know—was why I seemed to have been present when so many dead bodies were first discovered.

Before I'd finished processing this question, Aaron reappeared in the bathroom doorway. "Can you please find Ms. Weathers and let her know she's not to leave the premises before talking with me first."

The last thing I wanted to do was walk over to the billiard room to give Marigold any kind of directive, but I nodded, regardless. I would help in any way I could, even if doing so put me even more at odds with the queen witch herself.

By Aaron's grim expression, I thought I could at least surmise that I hadn't been wrong about seeing a dead body. After he disappeared back into the bathroom, I steeled my fists at my sides and marched down the hallway. As I got close, I could make out hushed voices.

"What if Matthew Kelsey did it?" Ruth's voice said.

Marigold's voice was louder. "You think Kelsey would have stashed a body in his own house? He wants our business. No, it had to be those church ladies. We need to talk to the other witches before the cops get to them. Make sure we all give the same story."

"Do you really think Kelsey needs our business?" Rachael's voice was timid, and I had to admit, I was surprised at her speaking up at all. But in recent months, as she'd become more proficient with her artwork, she'd gained some of the confidence she lacked from her meager magic skills. "And I thought you said he didn't really want to rent the mansion to us this year."

"That's only because he usually dealt with Lizzie. Her Good Witch of the North act would have worked better with his campaign slogan for mayor. He's worried that our playing up of the creepiness of the holiday is going to jeopardize votes from some of the followers of that new pastor."

She said this as though it was a flimsy reason, barely worth mentioning, but I had to take a few deep breaths at the disrespect Marigold still seemed to hold toward my Aunt Lizzie.

Still, Lizzie was gone. I couldn't bring her back, nor had I known her well enough to defend her character. The more important question here was if the witches might be overlooking a valid suspect in why a dead body had shown up in their haunted house. I'd have to learn more about this Matthew Kelsey. And maybe this new pastor as well.

I wanted the witches to get to a place where they'd trust the local police more. At least Aaron and Jay, who I knew were good at their jobs and had the best intentions for Crystal Cove at heart, even if they went about getting there in different ways.

But for the moment, it may have been up to me to help dig up further details. As I rounded the corner, all of the witches fell silent.

"Detective Thom is investigating," I said. At the last second, I had an idea of how to make it seem like I wasn't throwing all of the blame at Marigold. "And he's asked that none of you leave until he's had a chance to talk to you, as you were all on site this evening and he'd like your perspective."

Marigold looked at the door behind me, like she might try to escape through it.

But then she averted her eyes from me and let out a huff, making clear again that somehow she thought this was all my fault.

Chapter Five

I SPENT THE NEXT half hour in the hallway right outside the billiard room, close enough that the witches had to whisper to not be heard and far enough from the investigation that I had no idea what was going on with it.

I hoped that by staying near, the witches would eventually see me as being on their side and understand that I hadn't done anything to purposely hurt them.

But every time Marigold looked out the doorway at me, it was with a clear expression of distrust. At least that was better than the others, who wouldn't even glance my way.

When Aaron left the bathroom down the hall and headed my way, I pushed up from my seated position against the wall. This caught the attention of the witches, and they huddled around the doorway to the billiard room.

"What did you figure out?" The question was out of my mouth before I realized how inappropriate it was. Jay had become relaxed about sharing details of cases with me, and even allowing me to help investigate in some instances. Not so with Aaron Thom. His middle names might as well be by-the-book.

He ignored my question and turned to Marigold. "Ms. Weathers. Did you or one of your fundraising group have anything to do with the placement of that man in the bathtub?"

So it was definitely a man. That made me feel both better and worse.

"Of course not," Marigold said indignantly.

That wasn't enough for Aaron, though. He looked to Ruth, and then Rachael, and then the other witch whose name I didn't know. "And you, ladies?"

They all shook their heads, wide-eyed and innocent.

Before he could ask another question, Jay came racing through the outside doors toward us. He still wore his plaid shirt and jeans from earlier this evening and he looked extra casual beside Aaron in his full detective suit. "I just got done at the other scene, Thom. Now what can I do to help?" When his eyes flicked from Aaron to me, he did a double-take. "Tabby?"

I nodded. "This was the situation I called you about. When you were busy, I called Detective Thom right away." On instinct, I knew not to call Aaron by his first name here, especially with so much witchy scrutiny surrounding us.

Aaron didn't give Jay so much as a second to process this. He pulled him aside, and while I couldn't hear all of their conversation, I heard the words "morgue" and "five days" and "hysterical sister," before Jay nodded and rushed back toward the outside doors.

"Now, ladies…" Aaron turned his attention back to the witches, but this time his eyes skimmed over me as well. "I need to know every single person who had access to that bathroom since you took possession of the house to decorate it."

The other witches stared at Marigold until she waved a casual hand and answered. "We didn't even use that portion of the house. For all we know, that body was there long before we came in to plan our fundraiser." Even though she said the words with confidence, Marigold normally stayed in constant fluid motion, especially when she spoke, but now she'd gone stock still, making me suspect she was much more worried than she was letting on. "Is the man freshly dead, or has he been dead awhile?"

It was an interesting question. I looked to Aaron, who didn't seem in any hurry to let me contribute to the conversation.

He ignored her question the same way he had ignored mine. "I'll need you to list every person that you had helping at your fundraiser at any point tonight," Aaron said. He passed her an empty lined pad of paper and a pen. "First and last names wherever you can, and please make a separate list of all the people who attended your haunted house."

Marigold pulled back. "But there had to be over a hundred."

"I'm sure there was, Ms. Weathers." Without giving her time to respond, he spun on his heel and marched back toward the bathroom, the medical examiner, and the dead body.

When I turned back to the witches, Marigold had started her first list with the title of FUNDRAISER HELPERS at the top.

The first name she listed? TABITHA CHASE.

Chapter Six

I KEPT MY SIGH to myself as Marigold reluctantly listed her other witch friends. I noticed she kept Ruth and Rachael's names off of the list until she got near the end of what was turning into a really long list and she seemed to really be searching for names. Ruth, Rachael, and the other witch, whose name, judging from the list, was Greta, offered their help when they could, and by the time they were all really struggling for names, they had over thirty listed.

I hadn't seen nearly that many, and so I wondered if some had left earlier, and if that was information Aaron would want to know.

I opened my mouth to suggest this, but then thought better of saying anything that might make Marigold think I was slinging blame toward specific witches.

Marigold soon started on her second list, the attendees, and she had at least fifty names before Aaron came out of the bathroom again. He stood down the hall making a phone call and didn't approach right away.

Marigold had been making a point to ignore me, but as soon as I thought of a way to open the communication lines again and try to be a help to her, I took it.

"There was a realtor here from Eugene. It was after I took over the ticket booth. Apparently, he comes every year. Donny something-or-other, and his wife…"

Before I could mention that I hadn't caught her name, Marigold's eyes widened at me and she cut me off. "Donny and Charlotte Enns were here? Why didn't you mention this earlier, Tabitha? Clearly, they're the ones at fault for this!"

Her words were loud enough that Aaron hung up and headed our way.

"How do you figure?" I asked. They seemed like friendly people, and I would have noticed if they had tried to sneak a dead body in with their skull flashlight.

"Who are you talking about and what makes you think they were involved?" Aaron asked.

Marigold gave me a long look, before saying, "Shouldn't we be having this conversation in private, Detective?"

Even though I suspected Marigold was continually throwing me under the bus out of pure spite, I backed away with both hands up, like I was removing my hands from the whole thing. I was curious about the details, of course, but I had the feeling Aaron would be able to delve into anything Marigold may or may not know a lot easier if she wasn't distracted by her anger with me.

"Why don't you head on home, Tabitha," Aaron told me, giving me no choice in the matter. "I'll know where to find you if I have more questions."

I shook my head all the way into the night air. If Marigold had anything to say about it, she'd have the whole town turned against me by morning, and all because I'd stumbled upon a dead body and called the police about it!

I was so caught up in my whirling thoughts, I didn't notice Jay until he stepped into my path.

"Are you okay?" he asked. "I understand you were the one to find the body."

His voice oozed compassion and I was so taken off guard by his kindness, my eyes welled with tears. I looked around to where several officers were speaking to other witches and taking down statements. I hadn't seen any of them earlier. There had to be another exit through the basement. I forced a nod. "Yeah, I'm fine. I just… Marigold made me feel as though I'd done something wrong by calling the police."

"Marigold Weathers?" he asked. "She said that?"

Oh, great. Jay and I had become such good friends that I sometimes forgot he was a police detective first, with a job to do. And here I was trying even harder to make an enemy out of the town's queen witch.

I shook my head. "She was just worried about the bad publicity it might bring," I explained.

"Uh-huh." Jay pulled out his pad of paper and wrote something. "And Thom's talking to her now?"

I nodded. "I brought up the name of a guy I'd sold tickets to near the end of the night and then suddenly everyone wanted me to leave."

"What was the name?" Jay looked up from his notepad. I hesitated, but then reminded myself that competitiveness aside, Jay and Aaron were on the same team, both with the aim of bringing justice and peace to Crystal Cove.

"Donny Enns?" I asked as a question.

He showed immediate recognition. Then he glanced around at the surrounding officers. "Well, if publicity is her concern, I can understand why she didn't want to talk about Donny Enns. I'd better get in there." He motioned to the still-open doorway. "Go home and try and get some rest. I'll drop by tomorrow and let you know what we figure out."

I never would have expected him to include me on case details, but right from when I'd moved to Crystal Cove, Jay had seemed to trust me wholeheartedly. It most likely had to do with the close working relationship he'd had with Aunt Lizzie, but whatever the reason, I was glad I still had one person in town who believed I hadn't done anything wrong.

I thanked Jay and turned to head for my car, but then Jay stopped me with, "Hey, Tabby?" I turned back to see him holding a disgruntled-looking Sherlock up with one hand. "I think this is yours?" He winked.

I was tempted to leave Sherlock behind, and see if he could listen in about who this Donny Enns was and why he may have planted a real dead body in a haunted house.

But more than that, I didn't want to be alone after this crazy evening where I felt like I'd lost most of my friends. So I scooped up my cat and headed back to my houseboat for the night, where everyone thought I should be.

Chapter Seven

"I DON'T GET IT," I told my cat as soon as we were aboard the *Lady of Fortune*. I should have been getting ready for bed, but I was much too wound up for that. "Who was this Donny Enns person and why does Marigold think he would have killed someone in her haunted house?"

Sherlock was already nosing around Aunt Lizzie's detective novels, which I no longer bothered to re-shelve, but instead left in messy piles on the floor. He didn't answer me.

I took my agitated energy to my small kitchen table, opened my laptop, and pulled up a new spreadsheet. Since moving to Crystal Cove, every time I found myself near the outskirts of an unsolved mystery, I found it easier to think when I put all the information I had into practical organization. I chalked it up to the way my realtor brain had been trained.

It didn't take me long to type out every name and bit of information I could remember from the evening. I was leaning back in my chair in frustration at all the holes this left when Sherlock's nose against my shin made me look down.

"What's that?"

He had my chain and sea glass pendant hanging out of his mouth. I reached down and took it. I hadn't worn it tonight because it hadn't looked right with my outfit, but I had to admit, now I wished I hadn't put fashion first. While Sherlock's blue crystals helped him to communicate with me, sea glass felt more like my speed of magic. It helped me with my intuition but didn't feel so strong that I couldn't control it. I hadn't told anyone about it yet. Not Marigold. Not Jay. Not even Rachael.

I hoped that the second it was around my neck, something would make sense on the spreadsheet in front of me, but it still looked like nothing more than a list of names of people I mostly didn't know.

"What are we missing?" I asked Sherlock.

His answer came quickly, and even though it was vague, I also knew without a doubt, it was correct. *The history.*

My mind reeled with the possibilities, and my fingers flew over the keyboard as I jotted them down: The history of the Fright Night celebration in Crystal Cove. The history of Matthew Kelsey's mansion. The relationship between Kelsey and the witches. The relationship between Donny Enns and both the mansion owner and the witches. The tension between the witches and the church. And above all, how my Aunt Lizzie played into any of this history.

It gave me a lot to think about as Sherlock headed back to the detective novels. I picked up the one he had been nosing through, to see if it added any insight to the case. It was called Murder in New Orleans, and from the flap on the back, it seemed to be about a poisoning on a local food tour.

I flipped back to the page Sherlock had opened the book to and read a few paragraphs aloud, where the victim appeared to have been strangled by some Mardi Gras beads.

Even though I hadn't seen much of the man in the bathtub tonight, because of the dry ice, I'd seen his face and his neck. There had been rosemary sprigs around his head, but he hadn't appeared to have been strangled.

"I'm not sure this relates," I told my cat. "But let's start this one tonight in bed and see if there's anything else significant."

I looked in my aunt's full-length mirror before getting changed for bed and again regretted not wearing the sea glass necklace tonight. It didn't jive with my outfit, but who would have really noticed?

The Harvest Festival felt so long ago. I couldn't stop thinking about how much easier life had seemed only a handful of hours ago. After changing into my comfiest pajamas and washing off my makeup, I stepped closer to my bed, but my sea glass went instantly ice cold around my neck.

It shocked me so much I stepped away from the bed, but it didn't return to normal. Was I not supposed to go to bed yet? Was there something else I needed to learn about the case tonight?

I looked in the closet where earlier tonight I'd found the gingham dress, courtesy of my aunt's magical houseboat, which had ended up being the perfect costume to wear to the Harvest Festival. But now the closet only held all my regular clothes.

I headed back down to the main floor of the houseboat, and investigated every other area I'd experienced magical occurrences since moving aboard my aunt's boat. The yellow dish that I'd remembered breaking as a child was still good as new in the cupboard, but nothing else had changed. No new food had appeared in my cupboard or fridge.

I stared around the rest of the houseboat for several long seconds before my gaze landed on the door to the houseboat's cockpit, where I rarely ventured. The marina owner's nephew had tuned up all the mechanics of the boat when I'd first moved to town. The last time I'd been in the cockpit, it was to store a blue crystal that had belonged to my aunt. It seemed to have a strong unwieldy magic, magic I didn't feel ready for, but as my gaze lingered on the door, the sea glass around my neck warmed.

Maybe it was time.

I took a deep breath, fisted my hands and marched toward it. I was tired. I wanted to get some sleep and hopefully wake up with a clearer head, but it seemed my sea glass was steering me toward the blue crystal first. And now my curiosity was getting the better of me, because did the crystal have something to tell me?

I found it in the glovebox in a small translucent baggie, just as I'd left it. The moment it was between my hands, though, I didn't sense any special insight. If anything, the opposite occurred. My thoughts became scattered and fragmented, and I suddenly had no idea why I was even standing in the cockpit.

I put the crystal back down and my thoughts cleared enough to remember I had wanted to go to bed and get some sleep.

Sleep. That was the other area of this houseboat that sometimes seemed magical for me. More than once since moving in here I'd had dreams that had led me toward important clues.

Maybe that was it.

I steeled myself, focused hard on my intention of picking up the crystal and taking it to my aunt's cabin to keep beside the bed.

When I grabbed the crystal, this time I instinctively started counting aloud… "One, two, three, four…" as I took the crystal back to the living area of the houseboat, up the stairs, and into my aunt's bedroom. I was at seventeen before I placed it beside my aunt's bed, took my hand away, and could think clearly again. The counting had somehow helped me to focus.

Now I hoped the crystal's proximity would bring me the right dreams.

Unfortunately, it wasn't that easy. I tossed and turned through the night, feeling completely unrested when the clunking sound of mail through the boat's mail slot rattled me awake barely after nine.

I lay still for a moment, trying to remember any snippets of dreams I could recall from each time I woke in the night. The thing was, they weren't really dreams, just short flashes of images and words—mostly the word "Murder"—and images of the one horror movie that my older brother had once dared me into watching as a child. I thought I had blocked most of the movie out of my mind permanently, but in my dreams, I had clearly heard the word Murder spelled backward. Redrum.

These were not the clear kind of magical dreams I'd had in the past, and all I could chalk it up to was that the magic of the blue crystal was still too strong for my untrained mind.

I held my breath, counted aloud, and placed the crystal farther from the bed, in the closet. Again, when I let go, I felt a relief as my thoughts immediately became clearer.

The mail. Right. That was what had woken me.

Most of what I usually received in the mail were either local advertisements or bills, but my responsible nature made me push out of bed, thinking I'd better be on top of any business expenses for the surrounding houseboats. I was ultra conscientious when it came to these jobs, as running my property management business well was my one hope of proving myself capable to my father.

I stretched and then bent to touch my toes and grab for the small pile of mail at the same time. It was a heftier stack than normal, and I found a sturdy cardboard mailer from my mom within the stack.

Putting the others aside, I opened that one first. Mom and I talked a few times per week and texted almost daily, but I rarely received any snail mail from her. When I had the mailer open, a dozen photos slid out. At Jay's encouragement, I'd sent a few photos of myself in front of the *Lady of Fortune* to the organizers of my recent high school reunion. Even though I hadn't attended, the organizers had felt inclined to share a few photos back with me.

I grinned as I flipped through photo after photo of familiar faces, thankful to have moved on from my younger years when I'd felt like an incompetent outcast among my peers.

But looking at these photos brought on something unexpected. A sense of kinship, like every person in every single one of these photos had experienced hardship in the last ten years, too. Some, like me, had felt incompetent. Others held secrets they didn't want to share. I could see it on their faces, and I realized in that second how right Jay had been in telling me I had an ability to read people. It seemed even through photos I could do it.

I reached up to my neck, to see if my sea glass had warmed, but then remembered I'd taken it off last night and kept it in the closet while I had the blue crystal so close at hand.

I ran up the stairs to fetch my sea glass and had it around my neck before I sat before the photos once again. I picked them up one by one, to see if my intuitions got stronger regarding any of my classmates. The sea glass warmed, but all I sensed was a reassurance that my initial assessment had been correct.

"Huh," I said to myself as I slid the photos away. I felt bittersweet, half of me wishing I had attended the reunion, if for no other reason than so I could have proven to myself that my classmates weren't so different.

I read the short note from my mom. It held all the regular worries about my brother and sister. I wondered if she let her worries about me out when she spoke to them. I was guessing so. My sister was far too busy trying to catch up on school to worry about me or my mother and my brother hadn't taken a day off since graduating university, so I felt a weight of responsibility over my mom's emotional state. I looked around at her sister's small houseboat, trying to picture my mother here visiting.

"Meeow…" Sherlock caught my attention and I slid the photos and my mom's letter away on Aunt Lizzie's hutch before heading to the galley to dig out some kibble for him.

"Sleep well?" I asked as I poured it.

He stared up at me for an extra-long second before digging into his food. Although he didn't mind-speak to me in that moment, I could sense by his deadpan look that he was telling me: *About as well as you did, Tabby*.

By the time I'd brewed my morning cup of coffee, a knock sounded at my houseboat door. Sherlock and I automatically looked to each other, and then I strode quickly for the door and opened it.

Jay stood on the other side looking more haggard than I'd ever seen him. His blond hair stood up at odd angles. He still wore the same jeans and plaid shirt I'd seen him in at the Harvest Festival and then at the Kelsey mansion late last night.

"Long night?" I guess, pulling the door open wider for him to come in. Sherlock and I hadn't gotten home until well after midnight, so I couldn't imagine what time he had finished up.

Jay made a beeline for the galley and poured himself a cup of coffee. Rather than responding to the question that seemed too obvious for an answer, he turned and told me, "You'll be glad to know it's not another murder. Just a stolen body."

I tilted my head. "What do you mean?"

He motioned to the door. "Let's sit outside. If I don't get some sunlight, I'm going to fall asleep."

This was unusual behavior for Jay. He was forever wanting to hang out inside my aunt's houseboat, as if he might find some lingering magic from my Aunt Lizzie for himself. I'd tried to tell him more than once that he wasn't so far off with that, but it seemed every time I opened my mouth to do so, my brain went blank and my mouth dry.

I followed him out to the front deck and sat on a wrought-iron chair across from him with my own cup of coffee. "Where was the body stolen from?" I decided to get right to the point in case he did, indeed, fall asleep on me.

He took in a big breath and sighed it out. "The morgue. Our medical examiner recognized the body right away as one he'd weighed in on five days ago. A hiker who had been brought in from eating a poisoned mushroom." I recalled overhearing something about *five days* from Aaron's conversation with the medical examiner. "Curiously enough, Thom said the hiker's sister showed up at the station right after we identified the body, hysterically insisting it was no accident, but since there was no indication of foul play, he sent her on her way. It seems obvious it could only have been an accident—Thom said all the evidence pointed that way, and Mick agreed based on his examination of the body—but still, it's an odd coincidence, don't you think?"

"So how did this hiker end up in the haunted house?" I asked. I felt immediately annoyed that the word "murder" had kept me up half the night, and it had only been alluding to the sister's wild accusations.

"That's what we don't know. Marigold says she had nothing to do with it, but we have several witches claiming they'd seen the bathroom clean, without a dead body, earlier that evening when they had already finished decorating."

"So it couldn't have been the mansion owner, Matthew Kelsey?" I confirmed, mentally crossing him off my list.

"Matthew Kelsey? Why would he have put a dead body into his own tub?"

I shook my head. "I have no idea, but at first Marigold was trying to throw blame in his direction. It seems he didn't want to rent them the mansion this year. He had been more willing to deal with my Aunt Lizzie, so there may have been some tension there."

Jay made a note and said, "I'll look into it, but I suspect she was throwing blame anywhere she could, to get the focus off of the witches. Of course that makes it hard to believe anything she said in her statement."

"What did she tell you about that Donny Enns guy? Was he yet another misdirection?" Even though I knew it wasn't my place to pry about case details, I couldn't seem to help myself.

"I don't think so. As much as I can tell with her, I actually think she really believes he did it. Apparently, a few years ago Donny came to town and tried to bribe Marigold into making the Kelsey mansion appear truly haunted so that he'd put it up for sale. The deal went bad when he wouldn't pay Marigold and then spread details about her falsifying magic all over town. At least that's her story. We haven't connected with Mr. Enns yet, but Thom was headed to Eugene to speak with him today."

It was true, then. Marigold Weathers certainly did have a lot of enemies, and they went at least as far as Eugene, Oregon.

"So is he your prime suspect, then?" I asked. "Donny Enns? His wife's name was Charlotte," I told him, wanting to help in any way I could. "But I don't think she was involved. In fact, she was lovely to me."

"And Donny wasn't?" Jay asked.

I shrugged. "Just in a hurry to get inside. Apparently, he was eager to see the architecture."

"They didn't carry anything with them when they arrived?"

I shook my head. "Maybe a purse. Certainly nothing big enough to contain a body."

"And you didn't see them leave?" he asked.

I shook my head. "There must have been an exit through the basement."

"There was. Plus, one through the rear of the mansion. So it's safe to say you didn't really see anyone leave?" This seemed to point out that I couldn't be of much help at all. But then he asked, "What time do you figure Donny and Charlotte arrived to purchase tickets?"

"Not long before eleven," I guessed.

He took in a deep breath and let it out in a sigh. "Seems like too late to really have any effect on the haunted house. Unless they'd come by earlier as well." I recalled how Marigold indicated that several patrons went through the haunted house more than once. Before I could mention this, Jay went on, "And to be honest, I'm not sure I believe that this couple would drive all the way from Eugene to steal a body from the local morgue and put it in this guy's mansion. Especially when the owner wasn't even around for the weekend."

I hadn't thought about that. "Is that Matthew Kelsey's permanent home?"

"Yes, why?"

I shrugged. "I just wondered where he went for the weekend, how long he planned to be gone, how far away he was when this occurred."

Jay nodded, making notes. "All good questions, Tabby."

Sherlock rubbed up against my leg and the word *Motive* came clearly into my head. Could Donny Enns have been aiming to make the mansion appear haunted before Mr. Kelsey returned? It didn't seem likely, with no pyrotechnics set up, and only a body that was clearly stolen. Instead, I asked, "But who else would have had a motive to steal a dead body and put it into an unused area of the haunted house? I mean, most of the scary stuff was all in the basement, right?"

"That's another good question," Jay said.

But his eyes weren't on me. They were aimed straight at my intuitive cat.

Chapter Eight

AFTER COOKING UP SOME eggs and slices of ham, I sat down across from Jay and we made a list of suspects. He seemed impressed when I pulled up the spreadsheet I'd already started on my laptop.

"Does this list of Fright Night volunteers look comprehensive to you?" he asked, passing over the lined sheet of paper Marigold had written out the night before. It was nice not to feel her scrutiny as I looked it over now, even if my name was still at the top.

But I couldn't help. "Honestly, I didn't know half of these people were even there. Most of them must have been helping with the haunted house in the basement, and you said there was a basement exit?"

Jay nodded. "I understand you never made it to the basement? Part of the appeal of the witchy fundraisers are their theatrics. Many of them dress up and perform scary rituals for guests as they move between their gruesome decorations."

Now I wished I had ventured downstairs—for a lot of reasons, but mostly because I loved a good theatrical performance. "Huh. I thought it was all about creepy crawly spiders and jump scares, and I've never been good with those sorts of things."

I chuckled a little, but Jay was serious when he said, "The last time I went to one of their haunted houses was three years ago. I couldn't sleep properly for at least a week. They didn't include many of their rituals and theatrics back then, but they still had a way of making you feel as though someone or something followed you home. I think I would have preferred the jump scares."

I raised my eyebrows. Jay was usually intrigued by the mystical happenings in Crystal Cove. It was interesting to find something that stretched his boundaries of comfort.

This made me think of something else. "What about those ladies at the church? Mabel and Edith, was it?" I asked.

His forehead buckled. "What do you mean?"

"Weren't they trying to find a way to shut down the haunted house? Didn't they seem pretty angry about it? And they disappeared from the Harvest Festival for a while. Remember?"

He nodded slowly, and then pulled the lined paper back to himself to write. Not only did he add Mabel and Edith's names to the list of suspects, but he added another dozen names I didn't recognize. As he wrote, he explained. "There were a lot of church members who were angry about the haunted house. They'd been petitioning the mayor's office for weeks, but with the election coming up, Mayor Herschel didn't want to upset any one voting contingent in town." It reminded me of what I'd overheard about Matthew Kelsey from the witches. Jay went on. "I heard he even called our police captain to ask that we make an extra effort to keep the peace on Halloween night." Jay looked away uncomfortably. "I didn't want to say anything, but I was actually on duty last night. Undercover," he added. "My job was to keep an eye on the Harvest Festival and make sure I didn't see any groups planning anything like they did last year."

"Last year?" I asked, with my eyes wide. If you'd asked me right then, I'd have said we were very close to discovering the guilty party.

"Your Aunt Lizzie used to do a great job of keeping the peace between the church and the witches, but last fall they brought on a new pastor—Pastor Tony Moore. He didn't have much understanding about our local witch assembly and only saw them as an evil force in our town. Before she died, Lizzie was slowly getting him to come around, but not long after he was hired, Halloween was upon us, and a group of men from the church were so riled up by Pastor Tony's concerns, they snuck onto the Kelsey property and cut the outside power to the haunted house. The witches still continued with their haunted house, lighting candles throughout, but Marigold Weathers and some of her cohorts marched down to the police station the next day, wanting to find out who had been behind the incident so she could press charges."

"They did the same thing this year!" I said, only remembering it now. "When I showed up at the ticket booth, Marigold told me they had lost power, but I guess she'd learned all about how to work the main breaker panel since the last time, because she had it back on by the time I arrived. Did you find out which of the church men were behind it last year?" I asked, even more swept up in this town's crazy history. I eyed Sherlock, huddled under one of the wrought-iron chairs with both ears perked up. He'd been the one to suggest I look into the town's history.

Jay nibbled his lip. "Not officially."

"But you know?" I pressed.

He gave one slow nod. "That was another reason I was stationed at the Harvest Festival. To keep an eye on the people in question."

"And did you?" I asked.

He smirked. "Remember how Brady was at the fish pond and I said we had to catch the next hay ride, instead of waiting until later?"

Now that he mentioned it, I did remember that. Jay was usually so laid back, so I was surprised when we were suddenly on a schedule. I nodded.

"Bill Rustoff and Hal Morty were running the tractor at that point."

I squinted. "But you left so early? We both did," I said.

He nodded. "Detective Ross and I overlapped for half an hour. I briefed him in the bathroom before we left. It was a bit of a balancing act, since I couldn't tell anyone, even my sister, that I was on duty for the night. I had no excuse not to babysit."

He couldn't tell his sister, yet he was telling me. I couldn't get over how much he trusted me. I was learning more and more about the dynamics of the small police force in Crystal

Cove, though. There wasn't a lot of discussion and exploring of details that went on among the detectives. The senior detective, Aaron Thom, was naturally an internal processor. He barked directions at the others when he had a fully formed plan in his own head.

Jay was willing to admit he needed more than that to effectively solve cases. I was glad I was able to fill in some of the gaps. It made me feel more useful than I ever had.

"What about Pastor Tony Moore?" I asked. "Did you have eyes on him?"

Jay shook his head. "He's out of town, speaking at a conference near LA." He pulled out his phone and seconds later had the hosting church's website loaded. He flashed his screen my way so I could see the pastor listed as a special speaker this weekend.

I pointed. "Click on their Instagram. See if it's up to date with any photographic proof that he made it there." Maybe I was being nitpicky, but with all Jay had just told me, I wanted to be able to unequivocally clear at least one person from suspicion.

"Yup, this is him." Jay showed me his screen again, with a dozen posts from within the last fourteen hours." I let out my breath, but Jay was already onto his next suspects. "I still think Bill Rustoff and Hal Morty could use another round of questioning, regardless." And then he added the part that made me feel most useful of all. "Care to join me?"

Chapter Nine

ON THE DRIVE TOWARD the farm where the Harvest Festival had been held, Jay explained that the property was owned by Hal Morty. "I can't guarantee he'll be there today, but I'd rather catch him off his guard."

This made me remember something else I'd never heard any more about. "You went back to the farm last night, though, right? There was some kind of emergency?"

Jay sighed. "Yes. Remember that lady who'd come in as we were leaving?" I didn't recall until he described her further. "She was upset and wanting others to pray with her?"

"Oh, right," I said. She definitely seemed like she was ready to throw a fit if she couldn't find people to join her agenda.

"People tend to drive too fast out on King Road, as it leads out of town. The woman was upset and not paying attention, and well, she got hit by a car."

My eyes widened. "Is she okay?"

Jay nodded. "Thankfully, yes. She spent the night in the hospital with superficial injuries."

"No doubt. And all of this happened on top of the stuff at the haunted house?"

"Halloween is always a busy night for our police department." Jay let out a low humorless chuckle. "If anything, that woman and her accident may have kept the church folks distracted and too busy to interfere over at the haunted house. I'm just glad everyone was okay."

We arrived at the farm and had no trouble locating Hal. He was right where we'd been the night before, except the farm looked different now. More than half the hay bales had been removed, and the short stocky man was busy in the seat of his tractor, lifting two rectangular bales at a time from the "walls" onto a flatbed trailer. Another man was straightening the lines of bales once they were loaded.

"There they are." Jay waved both arms at the man on the tractor.

When he saw Jay, he moved two more hay bales before turning off the tractor and jumping down to meet us. "What can I do for ya, Jay?"

Even though it was a small town, I was always surprised for some reason when people knew each other on a first-name basis.

The man glanced at me, so I introduced myself. "Hi. I'm Tabitha Chase."

He looked at my outstretched hand and hesitated before shaking. "Hal Morty."

In an instant, I realized the reason for his hesitation. His hand was dirty, rough, and callused. I tried not to flinch as I shook his hand and then retracted mine quickly. He looked back at Jay in question. The other man kept working on the trailer.

"Have you heard about the incident last night?" Jay asked.

Hal looked much more comfortable in overalls than Brady had been. He dug his hands into his loose pockets. "We're just glad those visitors were all right."

Jay seemed to realize at the same time I did that he was referring to the *other* incident. "Actually, I meant the incident over at the haunted house."

His forehead creased as he waited for a response. Jay was great at asking open-ended questions and leaving long pauses to watch carefully as he performed interrogations. If I'd been running things, I probably would have already launched in with my next question, too uncomfortable with the tense silence.

Hal pulled his head back, like it had taken him several seconds to register what Jay was saying. "Haunted house?" He put his open hands up the sides. "No. I haven't heard anything. Whatever it is, I didn't do it. You hear anything about the haunted house last night, Bill?" he called to his friend, who I assumed was Bill Rustoff.

"Are you telling me that you and your friends didn't go anywhere near that side of town last night?" Jay sounded the slightest bit disbelieving. I couldn't imagine being a detective in a small town and having to hold this balance with people who called you by your first name. This wasn't even my line of work, and yet I could barely seem to hold my friendships with the local witches intact through various investigations. I'd have to find my own way to balance my desire to feel accepted in town with remaining true to my own moral code. So far, it hadn't come easily.

"All I can say is we were here all night." Hal jabbed his fists into the sides of his waist, standing up as tall as he could at his five feet eight-ish inches tall. "You saw us with your own eyes."

"That's right," Bill said, joining us. He was taller and beefier. They both looked like they were no strangers to hard farm work. "Do you think this Harvest Festival runs itself?"

"True." Jay nodded. "And can you vouch for all your friends? Were they all here last night, too?" Before he could answer, Jay added, "I know you've both had an ongoing feud with the witch faction of Crystal Cove."

Rather than answering, Hal asked his own questions. "What happened to them? What happened at their haunted house?"

Jay stood up straighter, too, practically towering over Hal. "For now, all I can tell you is that the events are under investigation. You're telling me you were both here at the farm all night last night? What about your son, Rand?"

Hal shook his head, looking assured as he said, "We were all here. I can promise you that. After a visit from that head witch, we were determined to keep our own place safe last night."

Jay raised his eyebrows. "You had a visit from a witch? From Marigold Weathers? When was this?" I was glad to see that sometimes Jay's eagerness got the better of him as well.

Hal huffed out a humorless laugh. "Two days ago. The Weathers woman said she was driving by and saw all this dry hay piled up.

Told me it would be a pity if someone lit a match. I knew she was just playing her power games, putting a little fear into us so we'd keep to ourselves this year." He shook his head. "I suppose it worked, because I told Bill we had to watch every inch of the farm for any signs of them last night. At least *we've* never attempted any destruction of property with them."

"And you didn't see any evidence of the witches?" Jay confirmed.

Now Hal raised his eyebrows. "When I saw you arrive, and then Detective Ross, I told Bill that any sign of a witch and we'd tell the cops right away. I even slept in the barn, looking over the place last night, just in case. How can you believe those witches are harmless when they make threats like that? That Weathers woman has too much drive for power and control at the best of times."

"But they didn't actually do anything?" Jay asked.

"No." Hal's answer was reluctant. "It was an empty threat. None of them ever showed. It used to be different when Lizzie was around. *They* used to be different," he added with a note of disdain.

Jay nodded and headed back toward his car. "All right. Thanks for the information, Hal. And you too, Bill. As always, let me know if either of you think of anything else that might be important. Any interactions you or any of the others from the Harvest Festival may have had with the witches."

I followed Jay to his car, thinking again of Mabel and Edith. They had left for a good long while after they'd given Jay an earful about the haunted house.

Even though everything Hal told us made Marigold sound guilty as anything, I hoped we weren't going to take his word for this simply because he and Jay had history together in this small town.

Chapter Ten

I FOLLOWED JAY BACK to his sedan. "Bill was pretty quiet."

"He's always quiet."

That didn't seem like a good enough answer to me, but I didn't have a chance to press him on it. We were getting in Jay's car to leave when his cell phone rang. I could tell Aaron was on the other end of the call by the way Jay only nodded, as though Aaron would be able to see him, without adding much of anything verbal to the conversation.

I had already gotten into the car beside him, but I was tempted to get out, to give him some privacy.

But would that be weird?

Weird or not, he might appreciate the gesture.

I had just reached for the door handle when he said into the phone, "I have Tabby with me. I'll bring her along." I started to shake my head, not wanting to be caught in between these two men in an investigation once again, but before I could say anything, Jay added, "Okay. Be right there."

I waited until he had hung up to ask, "Where are we meeting him?"

Jay spoke as though I wouldn't have been able to detect anything from his conversation. "That was Thom. He has some information about the case and wants to meet with me at Macklebees."

Macklebees was a diner on the highway to the south side of Crystal Cove. I'd never been there, but I had heard about it before, mostly from my detective friends. So it probably shouldn't have surprised me when we walked through the doors and the only faces I saw were ones I recognized from the police station.

I'd thought it was a restaurant or café, but it seemed more like an Irish pub, with a long bar and a million bottles of alcohol lining one wall, and weathered wooden tables and chairs grouped around the rest of the place.

Aaron was already there, sitting at the bar talking to a plainclothes officer I'd only ever seen in uniform before. When he saw us, he motioned to a table—empty other than the papers strewn on top.

Jay and I went to sit, but before Jay actually sat down, he asked me, "What can I get you to drink? Pop?"

I nodded, feeling out of my element. There were only a half a dozen people in the place, but it had a strange business-y vibe, like everyone was here to work, and not simply to enjoy a beverage or some pub food.

By the time Jay returned with a pop for each of us, Aaron left his conversation to join us. As usual, he didn't greet either of us, but got right down to business.

"I just got back from Eugene. Donny Enns is not our guy." He turned a paper on the table so Jay could see it. It was a flyer for an open house.

"No?" Jay asked. I zoomed in on the pertinent information. As someone who very recently worked as a real estate agent, I knew the ins and outs of these types of flyers.

"Just because it was advertised until eight o'clock, doesn't mean he was there until eight," I said. "He could have had a junior agent or an assistant close up." I snapped my mouth shut. I had quickly interjected because I knew this business so well, but equally as quickly realized it wasn't my place to speak. In fact, I was a little surprised Aaron hadn't told me to sit at another table.

"True," Aaron said, sounding unbothered by my intrusion. "But it turned out Donny closed this particular deal and the paperwork was filed at the credit union right before nine p.m. Donny proved that his signature was on everything. He could not have realistically gotten into Crystal Cove before ten-thirty or eleven."

I nodded. "That's around the time when I saw him."

"Right," Aaron agreed. "So clearly not enough time for him to break into the morgue with his wife, steal the body of Shep Whitley, and stow it in the Kelsey mansion."

"What about his motive?" Jay asked. "Did you ask him about his contention with Marigold Weathers?"

Aaron nodded. "I did. He said he wasn't the one who backed out on their deal last year. Apparently, Lizzie had been the one to call him and back out on Marigold's behalf. She said something about nothing good coming from dishonesty. He said Marigold started spreading rumors shortly after that about him trying to use underhanded methods to influence the real estate market. He had planned to avoid her at the haunted house this year if he could help it. His wife saw her in the basement, so they quickly headed for the exit. They were well on their way back to Eugene before the police arrived."

"Has anyone questioned Matthew Kelsey yet?" Jay asked, exactly what I had been wondering.

Aaron shook his head. "He'll be back in town shortly. I'm headed there next. In the meantime, I need you to check the morgue and the funeral home. The mortician is insisting the body was picked up by a disgruntled funeral home driver, and from what I can tell, the funeral home's driver said he came by to pick up the body, but was told it wasn't ready yet so he left. Sounds as though we might have something there."

"How did the man die?" I wanted to slap myself for continually interrupting, but I couldn't seem to help myself. After my haphazard sleep last night, I had to know that my flickers of dreams had been wrong.

Surprisingly, Aaron nodded and answered. "He was hiking in the nearby mountains and ate some poisonous mushrooms."

Right. I already knew that. I fingered my sea glass, for some reason feeling as though Aaron wasn't telling me the whole story.

He went on. "People who don't know what they're doing shouldn't be foraging for food." He sounded somewhat angry at the man for being careless, but I'd come to learn that this was just the way to see, if a person looked closely enough and from the right direction, that Aaron Thom actually had a really big heart.

Jay pulled at other papers on the table, scanning them quickly as though he knew what he was looking for. "And Mick said the time of death was five days ago?"

Aaron nodded. "Six now."

"So nothing suspicious there." Jay flipped to another paper.

"Well, yes and no." Aaron pulled a paper from the stack and turned it toward Jay. I had to admit, now that these two detectives weren't competing for my affections, they worked together fairly well. "Like I told you, there was a sister who had initially tried to report foul play. Also, there were some oddities Mick assured me weren't present when he first completed his External Examination Report. You'll want to check with the mortician about these as well." He pointed to a couple of handwritten lines on a photocopied report.

"Rosemary?" Jay's forehead creased with confusion. "This was stuffed in his mouth?"

Aaron nodded. "And around his head and on his chest."

"And these were not added by the mortician or the funeral home for any aesthetic reason?" Jay asked.

Aaron shuffled his papers together and stood, apparently done here. "That's for you to figure out."

Chapter Eleven

The Crystal Cove morgue was located in the basement of our tiny one-floor hospital. I'd visited the hospital once since moving to town when I'd brought Rachael in because of some stomach pains.

Right away this visit was different. Jay led me past the Emergency entrance and around the side of the brick building, down a slope to an unmarked set of double doors. Through the doors, we walked down a wide sterile hallway to another set of double doors, these made of metal.

The smell of formaldehyde immediately brought me back to the night before, and on instinct, I held my breath.

Jay pushed ahead through the double doors and even though I was frantically searching my mind for an excuse for why I shouldn't follow him, I couldn't come up with anything.

So a moment later, I found myself in the small one-room morgue. A stainless steel exam table sat in the middle of the room, but thankfully it was empty of any dead bodies. Along one wall were squares with handles, which I knew from my TV watching habits were likely coolers to store the bodies. I wondered if the man—Shep Whitley—that I'd seen the night before had already been returned to one of those compartments.

A man in a white smock faced away from us at a stainless steel table against the far wall, but he turned when he heard us enter.

He looked to be in his early thirties with eyebrows that were too dark to match his medium brown hair.

"Hello, there," Jay said easily, like being in a morgue didn't bother him in the least. "I'm Detective Jay Jameson from the Crystal Cove police. Is Dr. Gray in this afternoon?"

The guy shook his head. "He's not scheduled to be in the morgue until tomorrow."

Jay nodded. "And you are…?" Jay was good at asking leading questions that made people want to overshare in their answers.

"I'm Brad Coventry. I work as a diener here."

I wasn't familiar with the term "diener" and resisted the urge to pull out my phone and Google it.

"Were you on shift here last night?" Jay walked around the small room as he asked questions, as if inspecting every crevice and corner.

Brad Coventry shook his head. "I'm only part time. Going to school in Salem full time to get my degree." He seemed like an introvert, the way he didn't use more words than necessary.

"So you didn't come into the morgue last night?" Jay confirmed.

Brad shook his head.

"Was Dr. Gray in the morgue yesterday, to your knowledge?"

To this, Brad nodded. "That's why he called me in today. I guess he had to wait around here most of the day and evening yesterday to have a body picked up for the funeral home. He's home catching up on his rest."

"Why would he have had to wait all day for the funeral home? Aren't they right across town? Are they that busy?" Jay always had such smart questions.

Brad shrugged. "Not sure. Sometimes there's paperwork to tie up first. He asked if

I could come in and take care of the evening shift last night, but I was in class."

Jay fingered the handle to one of the compartments in the cooler wall. "Do you know the name of the body that was supposed to be picked up?"

Brad moved a foot sideways to where a computer came quickly to life with the jiggle of his mouse. He rubbed his chin. "Huh. I thought it was Shep Whitley but it looks as though he's still logged in here."

When Brad glanced over at the wall of coolers, Jay asked, "Shall we check?"

Brad moved over to Jay and reached for a handle on the cooler drawer. I backed up against the far wall, hoping the two men would block most of my view. But the second the drawer was open, I could see enough of the man's sunken flesh to bring me back to the night before.

"Yep, this is him." Brad was unbothered by the sight of the body. "I did the embalming work on this one."

"And can you tell me if this rosemary was your doing?" Jay motioned toward the dead man's face.

Brad screwed up his eyebrows. "Not mine, no. Who would do that?"

Jay glanced back at me. "That's what we need to find out. When was the last time you saw Mr. Whitley's body?"

Brad looked up, thinking. "My last shift was the day before yesterday. Thursday. He didn't have any rosemary on him then."

"You're sure about that?" Jay asked.

Brad let out a low chuckle. "Believe me, I would have noticed."

"And would Dr. Gray have had any reason to add this?"

Brad shrugged with one shoulder. "Sometimes family members make strange requests. When they come into sign off on or ID their loved ones' bodies, they ask us to do things. As long as it's not ethically objectionable, Dr. Gray usually obliges."

Jay nodded, glancing at the computer screen across the room. "Are you able to tell me if this was a request from a family member?"

Brad headed back for the computer and moments later said, "Not that I can see. But you should probably ask Dr. Gray."

I could tell by Jay's set jaw that he planned to do exactly that.

Chapter Twelve

AFTER LEAVING THE MORGUE, Jay called the mortician at home, but his wife answered and asked him to come by later in the afternoon, as her husband was having a nap. "He was at work really late last night."

Jay hung up, checked his paperwork for the case, and confirmed that Dr. Gray had returned to the morgue to store Shep Whitley's body into a cooler after one a.m. the night before. "Shall we visit the funeral home in the meantime?" he asked me.

I glanced over the seatback, where Sherlock appeared to be sleeping soundly, though the one ear that perked straight up told me he was listening to every word. "Sure. Do you know which one was supposed to pick him up?"

Jay smirked. "There's only one funeral home in Crystal Cove."

That made sense, but it surprised me, since there'd been three funeral homes within a mile of my apartment back in Portland. "What do you hope to find out? I mean, if he was never picked up."

Jay pulled onto the main road. "I'm not sure, but I got the feeling the records at the morgue aren't very thorough. According to Thom, someone there reported the body as having been picked up by the funeral home yesterday, but that wasn't in the computer. Brad Coventry didn't even seem to know what had happened with Shep Whitley's body last night. He didn't have any idea that the body had been taken from the morgue at all." Jay turned left, and I was surprised to see the Crystal Cove Funeral Home was little more than two blocks from the marina where I lived.

The reason I'd never noticed it was because, if not for the small sign, the place looked more like a two-story heritage home than any place of business I'd ever seen.

"Plus, if the funeral home was supposed to pick him up on the very night he turned up in a haunted mansion—that seems like an odd coincidence to me."

Odd indeed. I was simply glad that Jay was letting me come along for the ride. I hoped that when we finally solved this mystery, I'd be able to get the memories of the dead man's sunken eyes out of my mind.

Jay led the way through the front door of the funeral home. Because we were so close to the marina and I knew he could find his way home if he wanted to, I let Sherlock wander outside on the home's front lawn. I gave him one more look and a half-wave before following Jay inside.

The inside was spacious, with a high ceiling, and if not for the open casket right in front of us in the middle of the space, it might have felt like someone's oversized living room. Couches lined the walls and landscape artwork decorated the place tastefully. Through a set of double doors, I could see a small funeral hall with five wooden pews down each side of an aisle.

There was nobody in sight, so Jay cleared his throat, and said, "Excuse me? Mr. Monroe? Are you around somewhere?"

A smiling man with a full head of gray hair appeared from a rear hallway. "Oh, Detective Jameson? Hello there. To what do I owe this pleasure?"

Jay walked toward Mr. Monroe and I followed. "I'm at work on a case and I had a few questions." Unlike Aaron, who always seemed to wear his detective suit, Jay was in jeans and a dress shirt today. His casual attire made it difficult to know when he was officially on duty, but part of me wondered if that would work in a detective's favor.

As we walked past the casket, I was glad to see it was empty.

"What kind of case?" Mr. Monroe pursed his lips and jutted his head slightly, as though hearing better would help him understand. "And how on earth does it involve me?"

"Maybe it doesn't." Jay ran a hand along the smooth wood of the side of the casket. "What do you know about a Mr. Shep Whitley being delivered here to the funeral home?"

Mr. Monroe's eyebrows drew together, but only for a second. Then he let out a long sigh. "Well, I hate to say it, but that one's been a nightmare."

"How so?" Jay looked perfectly at ease, but I couldn't help my eyebrows from shooting up at this interesting answer.

"First, the morgue couldn't release the body until they tracked down a family member." Mr. Monroe counted off on his fingers. "Then they had a family member coming, but they missed signing some of the release papers. When the next of kin was set to arrive back to finish with the paperwork, I sent my guy with the hearse, but apparently he got there and was told the next of kin hadn't shown up. Poor guy missed out on a basketball game he'd been planning on attending out of town for it, too." Mr. Monroe shook his head.

"And is your driver around today?" Jay asked, looking around the small homey lobby.

"Conway? No, he's working at his second job out at the race track today. That kid's way too busy."

"How old is he?" I couldn't hold back the question as I tried to picture this "kid" that bounced between race cars and hearses.

"I think he just turned twenty-five." Mr. Monroe nodded with assurance, as though that wasn't only a few years younger than me and Jay.

"Right," Jay said, unbothered by or unnoticing about being referred to as practically a kid. "And so you are absolutely positive that Conway did not pick up the body of Shep Whitley last night?"

"Of course." Mr. Monroe headed back for the front door. "The hearse was back here by ten, empty." He motioned out the door to the large black hearse. "Feel free to check it over if you like."

I looked directly at the man. Jay had brought me along for this interview and so I figured he wouldn't mind me asking another question. "If Conway wanted to get to the game so badly, could you not have picked up the body in his place?"

Mr. Monroe laughed, and I wondered if I'd accidentally made some kind of an undertaker joke. But then he quickly cleared it up for me. "Believe me, I wish I could have. My last hearse bit the dust a couple of years ago. A funeral home in this area isn't exactly lucrative, and so the unexpected expense really put a crimp in business. I found the cheapest one I could—from Craigslist, would you believe—but of course the reason it was cheaper and why it hadn't sold immediately was because of its manual transmission."

"You don't drive a standard?" Jay asked.

Mr. Monroe laughed again. "Maybe when I was sixteen. But I'm too old for that. Plus, I've got a bad back and don't move as well as I used to. I hired a kid who's a good driver, good with cars in case this one breaks down, and can move any necessary supplies on his own or with the help of our friendly mortician." Mr. Monroe headed outside and tapped the top of the hearse with his hand.

Did he just refer to the bodies he received at his funeral home as "supplies?" That was when I noticed Sherlock nosing around the back wheel of the big car.

"All right, well, thank you for your help." Jay sounded like he was ready to end this conversation, but I suddenly had to insert myself into it.

"Actually, can we have a quick look inside the car?" I didn't know why, exactly. Except, what if there was a sprig of rosemary or something left in the back?

Both Jay and Mr. Monroe looked at me, stunned, for a long moment. But then Mr. Monroe said, "Of course," and turned back inside to retrieve his keys.

While he was gone, I nibbled at my lip, feeling Jay's stare on the side of my face. I couldn't exactly tell him that my cat's curiosity was what sparked this extra investigation of the man's car.

Then again, if anyone would believe something like that, it would certainly be Jay Jameson.

Mr. Monroe had left the door to the funeral home open and called from inside, "If I can find those darn keys!"

I poked my head through the open door, about to tell him not to worry about it. I had no idea what I was looking for after all, and even Sherlock had wandered off, quickly losing interest in the hearse.

But right inside the door, I found my cat. He meowed up at me from a nearby mail slot, beneath which I could see a set of keys, strapped to a bright green lanyard.

"Are these them?" I called, picking the keys up and jangling them.

Mr. Monroe appeared from his back office. "Oh, yes. There they are." He helped himself to the keys and headed outside to open the hearse for us.

He looked a little disconcerted by my desire to search the vehicle, so I told him, "I've never seen inside one of these before."

Jay, however, didn't make any apologies for his curiosity or investigative work. While I checked out the front end, which indeed had a manual transmission, Jay scoured the back end and even pulled out some evidence bags to pack up some sort of samples.

Sherlock was perched on the front step, right near the outside of the mail slot, watching us. That was what gave me another idea. I asked my question as I thought it. "If Conway returned the hearse around ten, why did he slip the keys through the mail slot? Were you not here to receive Shep Whitley's body?"

Mr. Monroe looked away uncomfortably. "Well, to be honest, I get tired earlier and earlier these days. I figured if Conway had that cute young girlfriend with him to take to the basketball game, she'd be able to help him transfer the body. Didn't turn out to be an issue anyway, since the body wasn't ready for pickup," he added, as though this would dismiss the fact that he'd expected Conway to get his girlfriend to help move a body. I shuddered at the thought, glad it hadn't been me on that particular date.

But while I was lost in the discomfort, Jay had another question. "So you can't guarantee that the hearse was delivered here empty, or that it was dropped off at ten o'clock?"

Mr. Monroe wrinkled his brow. "Conway's a good kid. He wouldn't have a reason to lie about it."

Maybe he would or maybe he wouldn't. I'd learned in my short time in Crystal Cove that anyone could lie, given a strong enough reason to do so.

Chapter Thirteen

"DID YOU FIND ANYTHING interesting in the back of the hearse? Any rosemary or anything?" We were barely out of the driveway when my questions started shooting out of my mouth. "Was it just me, or was there something odd about Mr. Monroe?"

Jay chuckled. "I find most people who deal with death all day long are a little…different. And I'm not sure I found anything of note in the hearse, but I could tell by your suggestion that you thought it was worth investigating, so I took a sample of a strand of hair and some of the debris caught in the felt. We'll see if the lab turns up anything interesting. Good call about questioning him over the keys in the mail slot, though."

I smiled inwardly at the praise.

I'd never been to the race track outside Crystal Cove, but it was one of those places that was talked about a fair amount at the café. Races took place every Sunday night. It was Saturday now, and I had no idea if there were special event races on other days. The race track was close enough to town that every Sunday evening I could hear the race cars all the way from the café, like clockwork.

Jay pulled into the large gravel parking lot, which held less than a dozen cars.

"It doesn't seem open today," I observed. "Does it?"

Jay shrugged and looked around as though he wasn't any more familiar with the location than I was. A wide building stretched the length of the parking lot in front of us, blocking our view of the race track. We got out of Jay's car, and before I shut my door, Sherlock hopped out behind me.

"Oh. You're coming, are you?" I looked from my squat cat up to Jay, wondering if it was okay, but he was already striding for the building.

I didn't stop Sherlock from scampering along behind me. Even with my sea glass, I still had little confidence in my own investigative abilities, and I often had more faith in my cat's.

Jay headed for what appeared to be the only door leading into the wide building, and once opened, I saw that it didn't seem to be much of a building at all, but rather a hallway between open-air bleachers that faced the racetrack.

The track wasn't small, in that it would have taken me a half-hour to walk around it, but

I could imagine a race car would take mere seconds to make the trek.

Speaking of race cars, there were a half a dozen of them lined up alongside the track not far from us. One was up on blocks with the legs of a man sticking out from underneath it. As that was the first person we'd seen, Jay headed straight for him.

Jay cleared his throat loudly, but the man under the car didn't react.

"Excuse me? Sir? We're looking for a Mr. Conway Martella."

Even though Mr. Monroe at the funeral home had not given Conway's last name, it was surprising me less and less when Jay knew information like this off of the top of his head. I was getting used to the small town life.

When the man under the car still didn't acknowledge us or react, Jay nudged the man's shoe with his foot.

The man quickly wheeled himself out from under the car and sat up. He was in his mid twenties with shaggy blond hair and grease stains all over his white T-shirt. He looked between Jay and me for a long moment before reaching to his ear and pulling out an ear bud.

"Who you lookin' for?" he asked in a loud voice, as though he was still talking over music.

"We're looking for you, Mr. Martella," Jay said. "I have a few questions, please, if you have a minute." It didn't sound like a question.

Conway sighed and pulled out his other ear bud. "What'd I do now?" He didn't attempt to stand, but rather sat propped up on his wheeling dolly. I was surprised at his resigned tone. I'd have to ask Jay later if this guy had been in trouble with the law before.

"I'm looking for a little information." Jay's voice was curt. "I understand you work for Mr. Monroe at Crystal Cove Funeral Home."

Conway sat up straighter. "That's right." His words sounded defensive. I watched him carefully to see if he was hiding something. Meanwhile, Sherlock had made his way around the race car, out of sight of Conway and sniffed around the rear wheels of his dolly.

"And can you tell me about what happened last night?"

Now he stood and shook his head roughly. "I didn't do nothing wrong. I swear. I did everything Monroe told me, and even missed most of my basketball game because of it."

Jay nodded. "I understand that. I'm still trying to figure out a timeline here, so why don't you walk me through what happened, exactly."

Conway's eyes were wide and he looked down at the pavement between us, as though he was searching his brain for what he might have done wrong. "Monroe called me at like five. He knows I got Fridays off, since I work late Saturdays and Sundays."

I glanced at Jay. That early in the evening didn't seem right.

Conway went on. "Drove the hearse all the way over to the hospital morgue, only for them to tell me the body couldn't get picked up yet."

"And so what did you do?" Jay asked.

Conway scrunched up his face. "I turned around and drove back to Monroe's. Told him the body wasn't ready to be moved."

"And that was it?" Jay's questions sounded far more relaxed than mine would have been. I fingered my sea glass trying to get a read on the guy, but it felt cool. Even if this Conway guy had made mistakes in his past, I didn't get the feeling he was lying to us now.

"I only *wish* that was it," he went on. "Monroe made me wait around while he called the mortician. Then he was supposed to call back right away, so I waited almost two hours. I was supposed to pick up my girlfriend and head for Salem if we were going to make the game."

"And this was at what time?" Jay made notes on his notepad, as he usually did. I didn't hear any suspicion behind his voice.

"After seven," he said. "Monroe finally told me to pick up Donna and then head to the morgue, and for sure the body would be ready be then."

"Wait, Donna? Donna Davine?" I snapped my mouth shut. Not only had I inserted myself in where I wasn't needed, as Jay was handling the investigation perfectly well on his own, but I'd gone ahead and filled in the answers to the question I was asking—the worst no-no when it came to interrogations. I couldn't help myself when it seemed he was dating one of the local witches.

Conway nodded, unaffected. "Yeah, Monroe figured I'd still make it to the game in plenty of time if I picked her up first. Donna doesn't love riding in the hearse, but otherwise, it woulda been out of my way to go back for her before heading for the game in Salem."

"And so Donna Davine was in the hearse with you when you returned to the morgue?" Jay asked.

"Yup. But would you believe the body *still* wasn't ready? They needed some family signature or something, and I said couldn't they get it at the funeral home, but the dude told me no way."

"The dude?" Jay asked.

"Yeah, Dr. Gray."

"And so what did you do?" I felt myself leaning closer as Jay asked this.

Conway chuckled. "While I was sitting in the car discussing it with Donna, we saw the dude cross the street to the coffee shop across from the hospital. He didn't even lock the door behind him and Donna said we should just take the body, since the guy was such a jerk about it." Conway laughed again.

Jay kept his voice even. "And is that what you decided to do?"

Conway raised an eyebrow and wiped his greasy hands on his jeans, still casual. "What, are you crazy? I don't wanna end up in jail again. We headed back to Monroe with the empty hearse. Even though I knew he wasn't gonna be happy about it, I chucked his keys through the mail slot so I didn't have to argue with him. I grabbed Donna and my own car, and we were out of there."

"Headed out of town toward Salem?" Jay confirmed.

Conway nodded.

"And it was what time by then?" Jay asked, making another note on his notepad.

"Almost nine o'clock. I shoulda known we wouldn't make much of the game, and that Donna would be crabby as anything about it."

"You're sure it wasn't closer to ten?" Jay asked. Mr. Monroe had told us ten, but then again, he hadn't been there when Conway returned. Or at least that's what he had said.

Conway rubbed at a grease stain on his thumb. "Nah. When Mr. Monroe talked to me this morning he assumed I waited until ten and missed the whole game. I didn't bother correcting him. I figured he hadn't heard me drive in, and there wasn't nothin' wrong in letting him think we'd waited that extra hour if it made him happier."

"Was your boss, Mr. Monroe, at the funeral home when you returned the hearse?" I asked.

Conway furrowed his brow, like this question hadn't occurred to him. "'Spose I don't know for sure. He parks out back, but it woulda been pretty rude of him to head home early when he was messing up our night so bad."

Pretty rude, but not illegal. By the set of his jaw, my question looked as though it had sparked some anger in Conway Martella.

Regardless, my sea glass was still cool between my fingers, and I was pretty sure I believed the guy.

Chapter Fourteen

By the time we got to the house of Dr. Gray, the mortician, he was awake, but his wife told us he had left for a meeting.

"At the hospital?" Jay asked.

"I assume so," she told us. She was in her mid fifties with graying hair and a frumpy cardigan over a loose wrinkled dress. "He didn't say much on his way out."

We thanked her and headed back for the morgue, but found that the same young man, Brad Coventry, was the only one around and he had not seen his boss, nor did he expect to for the rest of the day.

"Can I grab Dr. Gray's cell phone number from you?" Jay asked on our way out. "I'd really like to connect with him today."

Brad didn't hesitate to look the number up on his own phone and rattle it off to Jay, but when we arrived back at the parking lot and Jay dialed, it went straight to voicemail.

Jay left a quick message, hung up, and then looked at me. "It seems we're at a dead-end for today. Should I drop you back off at the marina?"

I was disappointed that he didn't suggest dinner together or sticking around to chat at the marina. I opened my mouth to say "Sure," but as I did, something else occurred to me. "Oh! I have to work." I checked the time and I could barely make it for my shift. I'd never *forgotten* about my job before.

"I'm going to need to go back to the station and brief Thom, and I'm sure this little guy is hungry." Sherlock had taken the driver's seat in our absence. Jay opened the door and ruffled his fur before he jumped over the seat into the back.

I kept a food bowl and some kibble at the café for Sherlock, but in truth, when working on a case, I was pretty sure my newly inherited cat could go for many hours, if not days without food or water.

When he pulled up outside The Heirloom Café, I searched for a reason to get Jay to come inside. "You haven't eaten anything in hours. Why don't you come in and grab a coffee and a sandwich?"

"I'd love to, Tabby, but Thom's already texted a handful of times. Easier if I catch up with him in person."

"Of course. Thanks for including me this afternoon." I picked up my cat and waved to him as he drove off.

Ten minutes later, Sherlock and I had both had a few bites of food to sustain us, and then he spent the rest of the day pacing behind the counter, while I made notes in my phone in between customers of the suspects who'd made an impression on me.

Bill Rustoff, the church guy who seemed too quiet.

Brad Coventry, the diener at the morgue, who seemed to be upfront about everything he knew. (I Googled *diener* and found it to be a morgue worker who handled, moved, and cleaned a corpse.)

Mr. Monroe, who had misjudged the timing of the dropping off of the hearse, and until I asked, seemed to be hiding the fact that he hadn't been at the funeral home.

Conway Martella, who hadn't seemed to raise any sea glass or Sherlock flags, but had admitted he'd considered stealing the body of Shep Whitley, and with his own account of the timeline, would have had time to do it. He also had a witch along with him who could certainly have gotten him into the haunted house. Not to mention, Conway appeared to have had run-ins with the law in the past. I hated to admit it, but he was looking like the most likely suspect.

By the time customers slowed down at the end of the evening, I was onto investigating Matthew Kelsey and his mansion. From what I could find on the Internet, he was a long time resident of Crystal Cove, and had run for mayor in the last election four years ago, but had been beat out by Mayor Herschel.

I found several online articles about his last campaign, but didn't notice much of interest until I saw two photos of him with my Aunt Lizzie. They smiled together, and in one photo, they both wore buttons that proclaimed: I SUPPORT KELSEY FOR MAYOR OF CRYSTAL COVE.

The interesting part, though, was that the word "Cove" had a large witch's hat sitting on top of it on the buttons. The other photo included not only my aunt, but also a dozen other witches I knew from town, all with buttons. Marigold wasn't in the photo, but Rachael, Ruth, and Donna Davine all were.

If I had to guess, these photos definitely suggested that Matthew Kelsey had the witches' support in Crystal Cove, and they had his support. At least four years ago, they did. Last night, Rachael had made it sound more like Mr. Kelsey had been trying to distance himself from the local witch crowd.

I looked up his current campaign, including the year with the search. While there were still plenty of photos and articles about his public appearances, when I skimmed through them and crossed my search with the word "witch," there were zero results.

By the time Olivia came to close up the café, I had a million questions rattling through my brain. But she seemed in a hurry to get home, so I kept them to myself, grabbed my cat, and carried him for the short walk back to the marina.

I hadn't heard from Jay all evening, and figured the only one I had to talk my questions through with would be Sherlock. I was lost in thought when I almost barreled into Frank, the owner of the marina.

"Oh! You're still here?" I asked at the same time as he said, "Just getting home from work?"

"Yes," I told him, and because my mind was still on it, I asked, "Hey, what do you know about a guy named Matthew Kelsey?" Frank had lived in Crystal Cove for several decades. He likely knew a lot more than I did about all of the locals.

"Kelsey? The guy ran for mayor last term. Think I heard he's running again."

I didn't need information I could easily find in newspaper headlines. "So if he's in politics, he probably has a pretty squeaky clean persona?" I knew from my dad's campaigning how easy it could be to sweep nasty rumors under the rug if you had a good publicist. However, I doubted the people in Crystal Cove employed good publicists.

"I don't know about squeaky clean. He's a bit of a player, if you ask me. Not married, and no one's seen the guy date in years. Rumor has it, he travels out of town regularly to hook up, where it won't influence his voting public."

"Why would going on a date influence his voting public?"

"I didn't say 'date'," Frank dropped his voice so he could barely be heard over the lapping waves. "Rumor is the guy pays for his companionship."

"He hires prostitutes?"

"I think he's cleaned up his act some since the last election. Or he keeps better secrets." Frank laughed under his breath, but his words only made me wonder if there were other secrets Matthew Kelsey may be keeping.

"How does he get along with the local witches?" I asked. "It doesn't seem like hiring a bit of female companionship would bother them too much."

Frank hitched his duffle bag higher on his shoulder, looking like he was ready to head home. "Not sure, really. I woulda said he was pretty chummy with them, but I dunno if that's the case since Lizzie died."

It was the same impression I'd gotten from Jay as well as from listening in on the witches last night. Lizzie seemed to have been a thread that tied this town together. It was definitely coming frayed at the edges, now that she was gone. This made me think of another area she had smoothed things over, and I wanted to ask Frank quickly before he left.

"What have you heard about tensions between the churchgoers in town and the witches?"

Frank raised his eyebrows. "Those detectives got you working on another case with them?"

I wondered if Frank was answering a question with a question because he didn't want to talk about this, or because he truly wanted to know. "Something like that," I told him.

He shrugged and started walking for the parking lot. "I'm not a churchgoer or a witch. I think you'd better go to the source on that one."

I watched Frank go and then headed back for the boat. I wanted to talk to Jay about all I'd learned, but because I didn't have any cold, hard evidence, I texted him a simple: **Drop by for a chat when you can.**

It was early the next day when my phone finally pinged with a reply.

Thom and I are headed back to Dr. Gray's house to wait for him. I don't like his avoidance. Talk to you later?

Avoidance? I didn't like that either, but I also didn't like the fact that there was no longer any room for a civilian to tag along on their investigation.

I texted back: **You bet!** in a peppier tone than I felt. Helping with investigations had made me feel useful for maybe the first time in my life. Even though I knew I had no right to ask to be involved, it wounded my fragile self worth to be left on the outskirts of one I'd been so closely involved with.

"I wish I knew how to help," I told my cat. "It seems as though we're at kind of a standstill. Although, it is a little strange how Jay can't seem to track down the mortician, right?" I pictured myself driving by Dr. Gray's house and waving to the two detectives on their stakeout. Or bringing them coffee.

I wouldn't do either of those things, but it made me feel a little less alone to imagine it.

Sherlock started pawing at a book, wanting me to open it. Truth be told, I wasn't sure much of what he'd pinpointed in my aunt's detective novel collection had been helpful in the past. But I couldn't deny that Sherlock was insightful. At the very least, he helped me to know which direction to go in next.

And apparently this morning was no different in that regard. Because I picked up the book and read at the back cover, where he'd pawed at it.

It turned out one of the main character's names was Donna.

And that made me realize who we could investigate while the detectives were looking for Dr. Gray.

At the very least, Sherlock and I could confirm Conway's story.

Chapter Fifteen

Donna always came into the café on Sundays, as she was trying to start a knitting club. Her group hadn't gotten a lot of traction yet, as the local witches were too busy practicing their magic to take up knitting, and many of the other locals shied away from involving themselves too closely with witches.

Again, I wondered if that would be different if Aunt Lizzie was still alive. More than that, I was starting to wonder if there was a necessary set of shoes for me to fill here in Crystal Cove, even if they were big ones.

I waited until my shift in the afternoon to talk to Donna, figuring it would seem more casual if I asked her some questions when she was on my turf than if I tracked her down at home.

After the day before, being wrapped up in investigating with Jay and then absorbed in my note-taking at the café, I was surprised at the buzz in the air as soon as I walked through the doors today.

It was shortly after one, and usually not many locals would sit in at this time in the afternoon, but there were at least a dozen patrons all leaning in to talk quietly across their tables. The buzz reminded me of the time right after a man had been found dead at the summer fair.

"What's with the busy Sunday afternoon?" I asked Olivia as I passed under the counter barrier to join her in the prep area.

"You haven't heard what happened at the haunted house Friday?" She raised an eyebrow. Olivia was always trying to warn me about getting too chummy with the police in town, but she seemed to know I ignored her advice and usually knew more than she did about local law-breaking.

"I did hear something…" I trailed off. It was getting to be habit to say less rather than more when talking about an investigation, and letting others fill in the blanks.

"So then you'll know if they arrested anyone for using that dead body to try and ruin the witches' fundraiser?"

It didn't surprise me that Olivia had been swayed onto the witches' side of things so quickly. They made up a big chunk of her business.

"That's the word around town, is it?" I answered a question with a question. Jay had taught me well.

"Well, sure." She finished wiping down the espresso grinder and rinsed her cloth. "Are you saying that isn't what happened?"

I guess I wasn't great at casual questions after all. I shrugged, trying again. "Who knows? I suppose it could have been anybody."

This seemed to relax her from giving me her studious side-eye. "I've got a new girl scheduled to train tonight. You okay taking care of that?"

I brightened. "You bet!" I'd been bugging Olivia to hire more staff for months. I often worked six evenings per week, and when the next busy houseboat season hit, likely for the Winter Solstice Festival, I would want time off to focus on that. I knew I'd feel guilty enough to try and do both if Olivia had no one else. "Who is she?"

"Her name's Katie. She's still in high school, so she'll need after school hours." That worked out perfectly, because I was the one who worked most afternoons and evenings. "Her family just moved to town."

I felt an automatic kinship with this Katie. Even though I'd lived in Crystal Cove for over six months, I still came across instances almost every week that made me feel like an outsider. Marigold blaming me for calling the police after finding the dead body was the most recent example, but even Jay knowing everyone in town by name, including his suspects, while I still had to introduce myself every time, reminded me that I didn't truly belong here yet. "Sounds great. What time can I expect her?"

Olivia explained how she'd fit this girl into the schedule and what she wanted her trained on today. I felt a wash of pride that Olivia trusted me with this. My boss could be a bit of a control freak, but I'd obviously proven myself enough to her that she would leave this responsibility to me.

After Olivia left, I brewed a pot of dark-roast coffee and walked around the café with it. While refills were not always free at the café, Olivia did this when she felt like it. She said it would get people to stay longer and order more snack food to go with their coffee. She was usually right. And today I wanted people to stick around so I could eavesdrop a little and hear if what Olivia said about Fright Night was indeed the general consensus around town.

I headed for the regulars first. They were comfortable in the café and didn't drop their voices as I arrived to top up their coffee. It took piecing together conversations from three different couples, but it seemed clear by those that Olivia was simply repeating back to me what others had been saying.

When I got to the table in the back where Jeff and Jolie were sitting, I stayed to chat for a minute, as the thirty-something couple had been really friendly with me since I first moved to town.

"How was your Halloween?" I asked. I didn't know for sure the couple's feelings on the holiday, but they were relaxed enough in general that I didn't expect them to take offense to me asking.

"It was low key," Jolie told me. "Jeff had to work, and by the time he got home, neither of us felt like gearing up to go to the haunted house. I suppose it was a good thing we didn't."

"Yeah, I'm hearing all kinds of crazy things about that night. What did you hear?" I held my breath, hoping my probing came across as simply a casual bystander.

But Jolie's brow crinkled. As did Jeff's. "Well, you were there, weren't you?" Jeff asked.

I nodded. Had Marigold thrown me under the bus that quickly? I pasted on a smile. "Oh, right. Yes. Helping out. It was a fundraiser after all, and I felt badly because I got there late, and to be honest, I usually can't handle much of the scary stuff." I wanted to slap a hand over my hyperactive mouth. "Yes" would have been sufficient.

"Word has it you were the one to find the body." Jeff raised his eyebrows, as if daring me to refute this.

Right. So not only had the witches spread the word about their innocence, they had made sure to drag my name all the way into it. That must have been why I'd felt such a strange vibe off of Olivia, and why she left so quickly.

Surely the locals didn't think I had something to do with putting the body there?

I figured the best I could do now was try to clear that up. "I came in at the end and offered to help clean up," I told them both honestly. "Because I didn't particularly want to venture into the really scary parts of the haunted house, I stayed to the upper floor, and that was why I was the one to find the body."

They looked at each other, but then nodded as if that made sense.

"Was he murdered?" Jolie asked in little more than a whisper.

The word reverberated through me, reminding me of my flashes of dreams the other night. Even though I wanted Jay to be able to trust my ability to stay quiet with case details, I figured it would help more than it would hurt, making sure a bit of the truth got out.

"No," I said, forming my words carefully. "The medical examiner recognized the body as one that had been brought to the morgue almost a week ago."

"So someone up and stole a dead body from the morgue?" Jeff's eyes widened.

I still didn't have any answer to this, so instead, I told them, "I've been working with the police to figure out who put the body there."

Jolie immediately leaned toward me and asked, "Really? Who do they think did it?"

I shook my head, more at myself than at them. I knew there was a reason I didn't usually tell people I helped with investigations. "I honestly couldn't tell you," I told her. "But is there any word around town? I'm sure they'd appreciate any suggestions of who they can interview next."

Jolie glanced at her husband before she answered me. "Well, if you listen to the witches, they certainly think someone had targeted their fundraiser—most likely someone who didn't like scary events or want any Halloween celebrations at all."

That wasn't terribly helpful. They were putting the blame back onto the church, or worse, me, and while I still had Bill Rustoff on my list of suspects, I was hoping for a more substantial reason to blame someone, or possibly the name of someone we hadn't thought of yet.

But then Jeff added, "I'm betting it was someone from the hospital—either a patient or a visitor." Jeff worked as a nurse at the hospital, so now I was the one leaning in. "Someone's been posting pamphlets all last month about how more casualties happen around Halloween than any other week of the year. Someone around the hospital was passionate enough about the subject to change the pamphlets a couple of times per week. Maybe passionate enough to do more than that, especially with the morgue right in the hospital basement."

It sounded more like a person who had been there throughout the whole month—a staff member, if you asked me. And I knew of at least one person who worked in the basement of the hospital whom we'd had trouble tracking down.

Dr. Gray.

I smiled, refilled Jeff and Jolie's coffees, and thanked them for sharing their thoughts, before turning to see the door open.

From the looks of the teenage girl who stood alone staring around the expanse of the café with a backpack slung over one shoulder, my charge had arrived.

Chapter Sixteen

"Katie?" I asked, striding up to her.

Her face brightened into an infections smile. "That's me! You must be Tabitha?"

I nodded. "But you can call me Tabby. Come on behind the counter. You can put your bag down and then I'll show you around."

Because I'd allowed myself to get distracted by delivering coffee and hearing local opinions about Friday night, I hadn't kept up on my usual tasks of making sandwiches. When a couple arrived through the door, followed by another few stragglers, I realized the afternoon rush was not going to make for the best training ground, especially when I was already behind.

At first, I suggested Katie shadow me, and I'd explain responsibilities more to her later, but after taking orders from five customers in a row, and then trying to assemble sandwiches and coffee all on my own, Katie was quick to jump to my assistance.

"Mayo, mustard, meat, and cheese on sliced croissants? I can do that," she told me.

Not only had Olivia hired a new employee, she'd found someone with some energy and initiative. I couldn't be happier. "All right, then. I'll be right over here making up their coffees if you need anything."

As the afternoon passed, Katie learned quickly. Before we were through the rush, she had a handle on grinding coffee beans, frothing milk, and making a wide variety of sandwiches from our menu—the ones I should have had already assembled in our baking display.

When the lineup slowed down, I had just started to teach her how to clean the espresso machine when Donna walked through the door. My eyes lingered on her as she took her bin of knitting supplies to the back upper level of the café. Katie must have noticed my pause in cleaning, because she said, "I think I've got the hang of it, if you want me to finish this up?"

Most of her sentences came out as questions, whether she meant them that way or not. But it gave me the ongoing sense that she was teachable and not only that, but willing to help.

"You're sure?" I asked.

"Of course?"

I looked at her for a long moment. So far today she had been nothing but competent.

And I really wanted to speak to Donna before any other knitters arrived.

I poured Donna a cup of earl grey, her usual, and quick-stepped to her table in the back.

I hadn't gotten to know Donna Davine very well since I'd moved to town, but she visited the café often. She usually came in a group of witches or she was busy prepping for knitting club.

She was really pretty, with long thick eyelashes and dark hair down to her waist. She garnered a lot of business at her spiritual souvenirs shop, and although I'd never been inside her store, I was willing to bet her trinkets were a dime a dozen, same as the ones in other local shops. I suspected people bought them from her, though, because in general beautiful people could sell you on almost anything.

Today she wore a colorful poncho—reds and blues and purples—which looked great against her dark hair. I had a feeling anything this tall lithe woman wore would look fashionable.

"I brought you a tea," I said as I stepped up to her table. But then I looked around because she had already emptied all of her knitting supplies onto two tables, leaving very little space.

"Oh, aren't you a dear." Donna was barely older than me, but her word choice and tone made her sound closer to middle aged. She cleared off several reams of yarn and took the tea from me. "I'll settle up with you for it in a jiff."

"On the house." I waved a hand and pulled out a chair to sit for a moment. "Listen, Donna, I wanted to ask you about something, if you have time?"

She stopped sorting through her knitting needles, placed them down and gave me her full attention. "Of course. What is it, dear?"

"It's about Friday night."

She tilted her head, looking like she had no clue what I was referring to.

"About what happened at Fright Night?"

She picked up her needles and starting to sort them again. "Oh, well, then I'm afraid I couldn't help you at all. I wasn't there this year." Her voice had taken on a standoffish tone.

I nodded. "I understand that. I also understand that you've been seeing Conway Martella and that you were on a date with him that evening?"

She let out something between a laugh and a sigh. "A date? Now that's stretching the truth."

"How so?"

She went on to explain how she'd been a big basketball fan since high school. When Conway told her he could get them tickets to the college championships in Salem, she jumped at the chance, even though she knew missing Fright Night would upset Marigold.

"And did it? Upset Marigold?" I asked.

This brought on a loud, hearty laugh. "She hasn't spoken a word to me since, which, believe me, is out of character from someone who can't keep her trap shut for five minutes. Truth be told, I hadn't wanted to do the haunted house this year, so I was looking for an excuse when Conway asked me to the game. Ever since Marigold's takeover of festivities like Fright Night, I've felt concerned about the direction she wants to take them—including séances and dark rituals, rather than providing a fun, harmless time for the community."

"Would you say that's changed since Lizzie's been gone?" I had to ask.

She nodded and met my eyes with sympathy in her gaze. "Lizzie certainly kept things civil around here. I heard Marigold even headed over to the farm last week and threatened Hal Morty!" She shook her head. "That's not like us. That's not who we are."

"Has anyone spoken to Marigold about these changes? Do you feel as though most of the local witches feel the same way?"

She shrugged. "There's no talking her out of anything, once she's convinced of it. I don't think any of us completely trust her anymore. I've heard she's been spending money like crazy. Rachael tells me she paid off her car and took a group of witches for a fancy dinner last night, of course without inviting me. So much for a fundraiser, huh? If you ask me, it's all kind of shady."

I made a mental note to drop by on Rachael and ask a few questions about this.

Donna changed the subject, before I could ask any more. "The worst part was, Conway had to do a pickup for his job on the way to the game."

I could sense distaste in her tone, so I asked about it. "You didn't want to join him for that?"

Her eyebrows shot up. "Who would? Believe me, I would never have chosen to accompany someone who delivers dead bodies for a living." She let out an obvious shiver.

"But you did Friday night?" I pushed.

She rolled her eyes. "Yes, and not only that, but he was taking so long in the morgue, he was going to make us late, so I ended up having to go in and fetch him." She let out another shiver, this one stronger. Conway hadn't mentioned that part. "We ended up barely making it to the game by halftime."

"So you did go to the game?" I confirmed.

With her knitting needles now placed in front of at least eight chairs between the two tables, which seemed hopeful considering her lack of participants in the past, she started sorting her yarn into colors and weights. "Like I said, half of it." She didn't sound happy about it.

"And can you tell me everything that you encountered when you were at the morgue?"

She shook her head at the table, clearly not wanting to remember the details. "Conway was annoyed, as was I. He was told he just had to do a quick pick up and then we could head to our game. We should have even had time to grab a quick bite."

She seemed to be able to belabor this point again and again. "But it wasn't a quick pick up at the morgue?"

She shook her head again. "I waited around for ages. First Dr. Gray told Conway there was a holdup with the signatures, so Conway came back out to the car and called his boss, to try and talk him into moving the delivery to the next day. While he was on the phone, I saw Dr. Gray leave and go to the coffee shop across the street, so after Conway was off the phone I suggested he go in, and see if we could get the job done." She held up her hands defensively, even though I hadn't said a word in accusation. "I know, I know, it wasn't a great idea, trying to go behind Dr. Gray's back like that, but the situation was ridiculous, and I didn't think it would hurt anything if the family had to come to the funeral home to sign the stupid papers instead of the morgue. All the back and forth was a waste of everyone's time! Conway and I argued about it for a while in the car, and our argument even got a little heated, but eventually I convinced him to go back inside."

 "So you did it? You took the body while Dr. Gray was gone?" Conway had been too concerned about getting into trouble to tell us this, but surely the police wouldn't charge him, if it was only the matter of getting a signature. Then again, the body hadn't ended up at the funeral home.

But Donna went on to say, "Unfortunately, a bald guy he didn't know was in there running the morgue. He must have shown up while Conway and I were quarreling. He told Conway he had to come back the next day for the pick up, and Conway was arguing with the guy when I came in to get him. I don't know all the details, only that plans changed and we were the ones who seemed to have gotten the raw end of the deal."

"So you did not leave with the body?" I confirmed.

She shook her head, eyes wide and honest.

"Do you have a name for the guy who was working at the morgue?" Brad Coventry wasn't bald, and they would have recognized Dr. Gray if he'd come back from the coffee shop. Interesting that Conway had mentioned Donna's suggestion of taking the body as something he'd never attempt, but it seemed he had made an effort to go through with exactly that. But he'd been stopped by another morgue employee. When Donna shook her head again, I added, "How about a description?"

This she could do. "He was in his thirties, really stocky, kind of a bodybuilder type. Bald with a goatee. And there was a woman with red hair, but she was working on a computer and didn't turn around to talk to us."

That was far from what Brad Coventry had looked like. And even though I'd never met him, I had a strange feeling it wasn't what Dr. Gray with the frumpy middle-aged wife looked like either, but I'd be sure to ask Jay about that later.

However, two people came to mind with those particular descriptions. And I'd seen them both at the Harvest Festival.

Chapter Seventeen

JAY DROPPED BY THE café later that afternoon. Between questioning Donna and the interspersed rush of patrons we got at the café, I hadn't had time to teach Katie much more, but the girl had a keen eye. Not only had she picked up a lot from shadowing me, she also noticed how my eyes lingered after Jay after he took a seat with his coffee.

"Is he your boyfriend?" she asked.

My cheeks warmed. "Oh no. Nothing like that. Just a friend."

"Well, he's a very good looking friend, if you ask me." She slid the bean holder back into the grinder and raised her eyebrows a couple of times with innuendo. "It's pretty slow right now. I think I can handle things here if you want to go talk to him?"

I shook my head. "You haven't even taken a break yet. Why don't you make yourself a tea or coffee and do that?" It took everything in me to offer this when all I wanted was to catch up with Jay.

"Ehh, I'm not really much for taking breaks." She said the words as though she had a lemon in her mouth. Sherlock wound around her legs. They'd both taken an immediate liking to one another—as long as Katie didn't attempt to pick him up. He didn't have a lot of patience with being held, unless it would somehow further an investigation or save him a long walk. "Even in school, it's much easier to keep working once I have some momentum."

A new employee who didn't want to take breaks? And she sends me to visit my friends while she takes over? Olivia had struck gold with this one.

I didn't argue anymore, but insisted she at least help herself to a drink while she tidied up. I took the coffee pot around to fill cups one more time before I finally stopped at Jay's table. It made it seem, at least to me, like I was still half-working.

"Who's the new girl?" he asked as I approached, motioning to where Katie had her back to us, cleaning up the sandwich prep area.

"New employee. Katie Johansen. She's great!" I wanted to get right to the point, in hopes of getting some real information about the case in the short time I had to chat. "Did you track down Dr. Gray?"

He nodded as I took a seat across from him. "I've confirmed that he was working alone in the morgue Friday night. He had no idea Shep Whitley's body had gone missing until Thom called him at home late that night."

"Working alone?" That didn't seem right. Donna had mentioned two other employees. But I started with this: "If he was on duty, how could someone have stolen a body from right under his nose?" Before I'd finished asking the question, a thought came to me. I spoke it before Jay could answer. "Didn't Conway say Dr. Gray left the morgue unattended to go across the street to a coffee shop? Who were his other employees?" I'd get to my full conversation with Donna later, but I suddenly wished I had pried a little harder into this point.

"No one, apparently," Jay told me, looking at the table in front of him. "And I understand he left it unattended for most of the evening, not just for a quick coffee."

"Well, where was he? Why has he been avoiding the police?" I was still confused about why Dr. Gray would say he left the morgue unattended when Donna said there was that bodybuilder fellow and the redheaded woman. But for the moment, I was more focused on where the doctor had vanished to. I guess a part of me was still eager to believe this mortician whom I'd never met might be responsible for the stolen body,

The deep breath that Jay took in and let out slowly only stoked the fire within me. He leaned in across the table. "He was with another woman," Jay told me in barely a whisper.

My eyebrows shot up. "Like an affair?"

Jay nodded. "We confirmed his whereabouts with his mistress, down the road from the hospital at her house. He also went to see her yesterday afternoon, when we thought he was avoiding talking to us. He was avoiding us, in a sense, but only to try to keep his affair under wraps."

"But he won't be able to now?" I guessed.

Jay shrugged. "I'm not about to take Mrs. Gray out for dinner to relay the details, but I also explained to him that the details from a case like this one could not be kept private when there was an ongoing investigation, especially if it eventually goes to trial. He planned to tell his wife himself."

"So he was headed back home?"

Jay shook his head and took a sip of his coffee, making me wait for the answer. "I requested a full autopsy in light of the rosemary that we found on the body of Shep Whitley. Neither Brad Coventry nor Dr. Gray claim they put it there, and there could be other clues we're missing."

"An autopsy wasn't done when he was first brought in?" I asked.

Jay shook his head. "His initial symptoms included a swollen tongue and mushroom remnants in his mouth. This type of poisoning is unfortunately common in these parts, and unless there's some question about the cause of death or suspected foul play, an autopsy is not usually done."

On the words "foul play" my mind ricocheted to my snippets of dreams from the other night. But rosemary sprigs, while weird, didn't indicate murder.

"Dr. Gray will be staying at the morgue with the forensic pathologist until he's able to give me a full report."

I kind of wished I'd been there for Jay's meeting with Dr. Gray, as it sounded like he'd put the man in his place.

"What about the other employees at the morgue, couldn't they have been responsible for the rosemary?"

Jay furrowed his brow. "No. Dr. Gray says Brad is his only employee at the morgue."

Now it was my turn to furrow my brow.

Jay asked, "Why? What did you find out?" to prod me into an explanation.

"I talked to Donna Davine earlier. She went into the morgue when her boyfriend was taking too long, and described a morgue worker much differently than Brad. She described a bodybuilder type, bald with dark goatee. And a woman with red hair, but she didn't see her face."

Jay pulled out his pad of paper and made a note of this. "I can't say I know anyone in town of that description."

"Apparently Conway didn't know him either. He wasn't one of the regular workers at the morgue."

Jay twisted his lips. "I suppose I'll have to pay Dr. Gray another visit and ask him about the description of these mysterious workers."

I hesitated, but then threw out another idea. "Or you could try your church friends?"

"What's that?" Jay looked confused.

"I think I saw a man of this description sitting in his car as we were about to leave the Harvest Festival. I didn't see him go in, but he had to be way out there for a reason, right?"

Jay nodded. "You're right."

"And remember that crazed woman that came to the festival wanting prayer?"

His eyes widened, but only for a second. "Red curly hair."

"Exactly." This part I wasn't as sure about, but I figured I'd better say it anyway. "The man looked nervous or agitated. At the time, I thought he didn't want to go into a social function alone. I've felt that way a lot of times. But I don't know. Maybe he was agitated about something else."

"Like having just stolen a body and left it in a haunted house?"

I shook my head. I suspected the timeline was too early for that, if Conway and Donna had seen him in the morgue right before nine. "Or maybe he left the Harvest Festival to go straight to the morgue."

Before Jay left to go back and speak with the church members who owned the farm where the Harvest Festival had been held, I told him more about my conversation with Donna. No one had ended up showing up for her knitting club and when she'd left, she was convinced that Marigold had turned the entire town against her. Unfortunately, I knew what that felt like.

"Donna said that Marigold Weathers has been strangely quiet and spending lots of money in the last couple of days. Apparently, yesterday she paid off a long-standing debt on her car. I thought about asking Rachael about it. I mean, if that's okay with you."

Jay nodded, standing with his empty cup. "Absolutely. Let me know what you hear." He put a hand on my shoulder. "I appreciate this information you've given me, Tabby."

Again, I felt useful in a way that I hadn't in my whole life before coming to Crystal Cove.

"I'm happy to help," I told him honestly. "Those witches can be protective of one another, but if I find out anything at all, I'll call you right away."

Chapter Eighteen

I CALLED RACHAEL TO see if she could drop by the café, but she said she was in bed with a head cold. She didn't sound terribly sick on the phone, and I mentally listed all the reasons I could think of why she might be avoiding me.

Maybe Marigold told her to.

Or she knew something about Friday night that she wanted to keep to herself.

Or she knew Marigold had done something wrong and wanted to protect her.

Before I came up with any other reasons, Katie called me over, needing some help with a specialty coffee order I hadn't taught her to make yet. By the time I was done demonstrating, we were into another rush that lasted until Olivia arrived back at the café to close up shop.

"How did it go?" Olivia looked between me and Katie.

Katie stared at me with what looked like bated breath, like she had no idea how well she had done. Then again, she was sixteen. How many jobs could she have had before this one?

I had no trouble answering Olivia. "You picked a winner, boss. Katie is exactly the hard-working, quick-learning girl we need around here."

Her face reddened, and she turned as if this was her cue to continue cleaning, even though it was all pretty much done at this point.

Olivia nodded. She wasn't usually one to show much in the way of pleased emotions. "One more shift with Tabitha and then you think you'll be ready to work on your own here, Katie?"

"I don't even think she needs that," I said at the same time as Katie said, "One more sounds good." I smiled and let her words stand. I'd be happy to work another shift with her.

I hadn't had much time to think about Rachael, so I hadn't decided what to do about her, or if it was too late to do anything tonight, as it was already after ten.

Katie interrupted my thoughts as Olivia headed through to the back room. "Any chance I can catch a ride home with you? Then I wouldn't have to call my parents."

"Oh. Uh, sure." Of course I was happy to help, but I wasn't sure how to explain to the girl how close I lived, and that we'd actually have to go and get my car from the marina first. I was always wide awake after shifts at the café, though, so I was more than happy to oblige, and if her place happened to be anywhere near Rachael's, who knew, maybe I'd even drop in on her and confront that problem before it rattled around in my mind, creating more questions through the night.

I could have asked Olivia to take Katie home, as it was more likely they'd be going the same direction, but I also felt badly that I'd spent all day talking and thinking about the case with Donna and Jay and I really hadn't asked Katie much about herself.

As Olivia locked the café's front door and headed for her car, I motioned with my head and walked the other direction, with Sherlock scampering along behind me. "Come on, my car is this way." As soon as she caught up to me, I said, "So I haven't heard anything about you yet. Olivia said you just moved to Crystal Cove? Where did you move from?"

She sighed. "A small town in Ohio. My dad wants to retire by the ocean."

My eyebrows shot up. "Retire? How old is he?"

She nodded and smiled, like she'd gotten this question many times. "My parents are both in their sixties. My dad has had a couple of heart attacks and has really high blood pressure. My mom will probably still work, if she can find a job in town."

I did the mental math. They would have had to have had her in their mid-forties for them to both be in their sixties. I wondered if she was an unplanned child. But I wasn't about to ask that, so instead, I asked, "Do you have brothers and sisters?"

She nodded. "Yeah, four. But they're spread all over the states. They're in their thirties."

That pretty much answered my unasked question. "Sounds like you miss Ohio."

She gave a half-smile. "Not so much. High school was pretty rough in my town. I'm hoping for a fresh start here."

"Rough? Like you were bullied?"

She shrugged in a way that seemed as though she was agreeing but didn't want to say so. And I supposed with such elderly parents, they might not have had the energy to protect her or help her through it.

I didn't know many teenagers from town. They came into the café, of course, but they never stuck around with their coffee and they never had lengthy conversations with the baristas. I hoped Katie wasn't walking into a similar situation in Crystal Cove. But at least here she had me. I'd only met the girl a few hours ago, but I already knew that if I caught wind of anyone treating her badly I wouldn't be able to stand idly by. Plus, I had two detective friends who might be willing to help make sure a young newcomer felt safe.

"Why do you park way down here?" she asked with a raised eyebrow as I unlocked my car for her.

I thought fast, but also wanted to be truthful. "Actually, I live here." I pointed toward the rear wharf. "On my late aunt's houseboat. I also manage houseboat rentals in the tourist season." She opened her mouth, confusion evident on her face, but I cut her off before she could ask why on earth I'd said I could drive her home. "I wanted to drop in on a friend across town, so it's really no problem to give you a lift."

She checked the time on her phone. "At ten-thirty at night? Are you being straight with me?"

In an effort to do exactly that, I told her the truth. I figured it might calm me down to get this off my chest anyway. "This friend…she said she was sick, but…" I trailed off, having a hunch she would understand all about lying friends.

"But you don't think she is sick? So you're going to drop in on her and see?"

I nodded.

Now she motioned toward the rear wharf. "You got any soup on that houseboat of yours?"

I narrowed my eyes. I'd made a big pot of soup two days ago that I was still making my way through, but how did she know that? "Yessss."

She smirked. "If you drop by trying to catch her in a lie, you have to have a reason." She let that sink in for a second before asking, "You know?"

I did know. What she said made perfect sense. If I walked up to Rachael's door empty-handed at ten-thirty at night, even if her lights were on, it could put some strain on our friendship. Especially if she was indeed avoiding me or lying about being sick.

"You're pretty smart, you know that?" I said as I led the way down the wharf to my houseboat to pack up some soup.

"I know," she told me. "Now why don't you tell me why you think this friend of yours would lie to you about being sick?"

Chapter Nineteen

By the time Katie and I were back in my car with soup packed up, I had explained the vague details of the gossip of what had transpired at the haunted house two nights earlier.

"And so you think this Marigold person is hiding something? And you think your friend Rachael is covering for her?" Katie had no trouble condensing the whole story into two concise sentences.

"That's about the gist of it, yeah."

She nodded. "I think you should take me with you. To visit your friend Rachael. Before you drop me off." She added each bit until my face showed some understanding.

"Why?" And how would I explain bringing a stranger to Rachael's apartment at what was now turning into closer to eleven o'clock at night?

Katie sat back into her seat. "I can read people. It's the one thing I've always been good at."

I'd say there were plenty more things this girl was good at, but if this was a skill she had no trouble seeing in herself, who was I to argue? Not to mention, it gave us something else in common. I looked forward to seeing if my read on Rachael matched Katie's.

I gave Katie a side-eyed look, wondering how receptive she would be to hearing about my strange sea glass and even the blue crystal I kept aboard Aunt Lizzie's boat.

But that was for another day.

We arrived at Rachael's apartment, and sure enough her lights were on inside. Not only that, but Marigold's long brown sedan sat outside in the driveway.

"Marigold is here." I stared up toward the apartment. "I guess we can't drop in on her after all."

"Why not?" Katie reached over the seat to retrieve my sealable container from beside Sherlock. "We're just delivering soup. Besides, why not get a sense off of this Marigold person at the same time?"

I had to admit, if Katie had been this ready to get into people's stuff back in Ohio, I could see why she might have come up against some opposition. But I wanted to be able to get some answers tonight, and I was much happier not to have to try and get them alone.

Thirty seconds later, Katie and I stood at Rachael's second-floor apartment door, knocking. The door whipped quickly open, with Marigold standing on the other side. She had her coat on, like she was getting ready to leave. Her brow contracted deeply at us.

"Tabitha? What on earth?" She looked between me and Katie.

I worked at forcing a surprised look onto my own face. "Marigold? What are you doing here?" I had no idea what else to do or say. I hoped Katie only needed a few seconds to get a "read" off of someone, and in way of stalling for that few seconds, I introduced her. "This is Katie. She recently moved to town and is working as a barista at the café."

Marigold looked momentarily torn between offering up a gracious welcome to a newcomer and grilling me more about showing up at Rachael's apartment without warning. Marigold's stocky body blocked most of the doorway. She looked over her shoulder in what must have been Rachael's direction and said, "Tabitha and Katie dropped by?" It sounded like a question, like she was asking Rachael if she had planned this.

To my surprise, Katie inserted herself into the conversation. "Is Rachael feeling any better?" Her voice oozed compassion. "That's so nice of you to come over to take care of her." She stretched the soup toward Marigold. "Tabby told me how awful she was feeling, and so I made up my grandma's special healing recipe for soup while things were slow at the café tonight."

Her words sounded perfectly genuine. I almost believed her.

"Oh. Well. Um." Marigold seemed flustered, something I had never witnessed before. "She's really not well." Marigold reached for the soup. "Why don't you leave this with me and I'll put it into her fridge for tomorrow."

"Are you sure I couldn't just heat it up for her real quick?" Katie asked. This girl never ceased to surprise me. She'd never met these people, and yet she seemed dauntless when it came to pushing them. Then again, maybe that was exactly where her boldness came from. "It really will make her feel better. I'm sure of it."

I wondered if it was Katie's age that made her seem extra genuine. Whatever the case, Marigold sighed, looked over her shoulder one more time at Rachael, and then opened the door wider.

As we moved through the door into Rachael's small one-bedroom apartment, Rachael sank down onto her bed. Seconds later, her blankets were over her, even though she was fully clothed in her short black dress and black-and-white striped tights. She let out a cough that sounded forced. Rachael had never been much of an actress. It was why everyone in town knew all about her lack of confidence when it came to magic. I didn't need Katie's intuitiveness or my sea glass to tell me she was definitely faking her sickness.

Katie ignored the fake cough and strode for the kitchen with the soup. I headed for Rachael's bed and sat on the edge of it, reaching for her forehead, as if to check for a fever.

"I wouldn't get too close if I were you," Marigold told me.

I smiled, but didn't retreat. I wasn't afraid of Rachael's fake cold.

"Were you over here all evening to take care of her?" Katie asked Marigold, in again what sounded to be the most genuine question.

Katie's question caught Marigold in a yawn she was trying to hide. I jumped on this, learning quickly from Katie in how to sound heartfelt.

"You look exhausted, Marigold. Go get some sleep. We'll make sure Rachael gets a few bites of soup and gets off to sleep right away."

Marigold looked from Katie to me, and finally to Rachael. She opened her mouth, but the woman I'd come to know always had something to say, didn't seem to have a single word in reply. Her eyes lingered on Rachael before she said, "You'll call me the second you need anything." It sounded more like a command than a nicety.

Rachael nodded to this and seconds later, Marigold headed out the door.

I gnawed at my lip as Katie finished heating the soup. She'd found a pot and a spoon and a bowl in Rachael's cupboards without having to stop the conversation at all. I had full confidence that she had also been studying the two witches with the eyes in the back of her head that she probably had.

"I'm so glad I had time to make you some soup," Katie said, as the strained silence stretched out. I'd already checked Rachael for a fever, and as I didn't know what else to do,

I lifted her wrist, as if to check her pulse. "It's never much fun being sick, is it?"

"Actually, I'm feeling much better than I was earlier," Rachael told us both.

"Maybe that's because your purple-haired friend finally left." Katie laughed as though this was a joke, but I wondered if there was some truth to it.

"Actually, now that she's gone, all I want to do is get some sleep." Even though I didn't doubt this was true, the jitteriness behind Rachael's tone made me feel as though we were making her equally nervous.

"Don't worry," Katie said. "We'll be out of here in a jiffy. I'll bet you're still shaken up over what happened the other night?" Katie stirred the soup casually as she brought up this topic. "The nervous system can wreak havoc on our immune systems. That's what my grandma always told me."

Rachael held her own grandmother in high regard, so I didn't doubt Katie's words would put her at ease. "Yeah, it was pretty crazy all right."

"Hey, you don't know if there was a bald guy with a goatee at the haunted house the other night, by any chance?" I asked the question as it came to me. "Or do you know anyone like that around town?"

Rachael shook her head. "Why? Is that who they're looking for now?"

I fiddled with my sea glass, which wasn't warm or cold. Rachael was being truthful. It wasn't my place to answer this, of course, but I was glad to hear Rachael wasn't somehow associated with this guy. "I'm not sure. I saw this guy at the Harvest Festival, and he'd looked a little jumpy."

Rachael nodded quickly. "Those church people really have it in for the witches. You know they cut the power to our haunted house last year. And then they did it again this year?" As she said the words, my sea glass went ice cold around my neck. She looked away as she added, "It was a good thing Marigold spent the last year learning all about the electrical meter at the Kelsey mansion. So she could turn it all back on."

Before I could respond, Katie said, "Wow, you really sound a lot better. I don't even know if you need grandma's soup anymore, but try some anyway." She brought a bowl of steaming soup over to Rachael's bedside. She passed it to me, I guess so I could feed it to her, and then took a seat on Rachael's nearby beanbag chair.

I didn't want us to get off topic, though. As I spooned a scoop of soup toward Rachael's mouth, I said, "I kind of feel like Marigold has been jumpy since Friday night, too."

Rachael sputtered at her soup. "Are you kidding? Marigold is always jumpy about something."

But this was untrue. Marigold didn't get "jumpy." Aggravated, yes, but not jumpy.

"I noticed there was a lot of cash in her cashbox Friday night. She must be happy about that. And I even heard she took a bunch of witches for dinner and paid off her car?"

Rachael turned her worried eyes up to mine. A second later, my sea glass followed with its own intuitiveness, warming against my collarbone.

I dropped my voice. "You can tell me, Rachael."

Rachael eyed Katie.

Katie popped up out of her beanbag chair. "Can I have your keys, Tabby? I'm going to go make sure that Sherlock's okay."

We'd brought my cat along for the ride. Katie loved cats and didn't argue one bit when I told her Sherlock enjoyed car rides and usually hung out at the café when I was working. But I had the sense she was only excusing herself, in the hopes that I might get Rachael talking if we were left on our own.

The instant Katie was out the door, I turned back to Rachael. "I know you know something. I can see it's eating you up." I took her hand in mine. "You don't have to carry any secrets alone, Rachael. You can trust me."

I felt a little duplicitous, saying this. Whatever she told me, I would most definitely relay to Jay, but I knew Rachael had not stolen the body of Shep Whitley. She'd been as surprised to see it there as I was. I was also pretty sure she was protecting Marigold about something. I guess what I really meant was that she could trust me to do what was best for her, even if that meant betraying her secret—or rather, Marigold's secret—to Jay.

"Did Marigold have something to do with that dead body?"

Rachael's gaze dropped to her lap. I sucked in a breath. I didn't think I'd really believed that could be true until this second.

"Did she steal it from the morgue?" I pushed.

Rachael's gaze shot up to me. "What? No! I mean, she said she'd try and help, and maybe she said it with more confidence than she should have, but she had nothing to do with *stealing* it! She didn't even know it had come from the morgue, not until after Detective Thom told us!"

I rubbed my forehead. If Marigold wasn't guilty of stealing it, what was she guilty of? "What did she say she'd help with?"

I'd put the soup down on Rachael's bedside table, but she snatched it up and scooped spoonful after spoonful of the hot soup into her mouth.

"Rachael…?"

She stopped scooping and swallowed. "She didn't have anything to do with stealing the body and it wasn't even supposed to be there until midnight. But those people showed up with it at like nine o'clock, and so that's why Marigold had to flip off the power and tell the witches to stay downstairs. Midnight was when she said she'd try to communicate with him. Then when they brought him early, Marigold couldn't get them to leave at first, even though we still had people coming through the Haunted House. She finally got rid of them by telling them to go and get more money and *then* she'd try to raise him from the dead."

My mouth went dry. Was Rachael serious? There were so many things to ask, I didn't know where to start. "Raise…who?" I had to actually hear it.

She nodded. "The dead guy. Shep Whitley."

Which Marigold had promised with too much confidence. "Who did Marigold tell this to? Who did she make this confident promise to?"

My mind reeled when Rachael shrugged and gave me a one word answer that stirred familiarity. "Carla?"

Carla was the high-strung woman who'd showed up at the Harvest Festival. She had been desperate to get prayer for her brother. And I was willing to bet this was the same red-haired woman Donna had seen at the morgue. "Carla's brother was dead," I said, speaking it aloud as I put it together. "And she came to Marigold to get her to try and talk to his spirit?"

I was still overwhelmed by the idea of Marigold trying to raise a man from the dead. Had she tried that before with anyone? Did she actually think she could do it, or was she scamming Carla for more money? When

Rachael nodded sheepishly, I had to ask, "Was she with someone? A stocky bald man?"

"I don't know," Rachael said. "Marigold only told me about Carla, and she only told me because I kept asking too many questions."

"But I don't get it. Why is Marigold protecting this woman named Carla?"

The worried look crossed Rachael's face again. "Because Carla paid Marigold ten thousand dollars that night."

"And Marigold doesn't want to give it back?" I guessed.

"She can't." Rachael looked like she was about to cry, as if this was something she, herself, had done. "She already spent it."

Chapter Twenty

THAT NIGHT, EVEN WITH my blue crystal tucked away in the closet, I had a montage of similar dreams with a flash of the word "Murder." But this time, I sat straight up in the middle of the night, a sudden thought hitting me.

Didn't Jay tell me about the hiker's sister insisting to Aaron that her brother was murdered? If this sister was the very same Carla who visited the church and then Marigold, and she truly believed her brother had been murdered, it made sense why she might have been desperate to contact him in any way she could, if she had been dismissed by the police.

Even though I had left Jay a long-winded message when I got back to the houseboat, I grabbed for my phone and left him another. I didn't hear back from him until early in the morning. I'd left my phone on in case he called, and the ringer startled both me and Sherlock awake.

"Hello?" I said, out of breath from the startling. It felt as though I'd barely fallen back to sleep.

"I got your messages. Anything else I should know before heading out to the Morty farm to question them about Carla Whitley?"

Sherlock crawled onto my lap and pawed at my phone. His forwardness spurred me on with the courage to ask, "Can I tag along? You know, in case I forgot to mention anything."

A pause and then, "You're sure you're up for it? I wanted to get there as soon as possible.

There's a farmer's market today, and I want to catch Hal out in the field before he heads there."

As I moved off my bed, Sherlock dodged off my lap and toward the door. He was planning to get ready as quickly as I was. "Give me ten minutes."

I jogged toward the marina parking lot nine minutes later with Sherlock in my arms and my hair still wet from the shower. I was not about to make Jay any later, no matter how I looked doing it.

When he hadn't yet arrived, I pulled a compact out of my purse and did what I could to scrunch my hair gel and give it a little lift. I was just applying a little lip gloss and concealer to hide my eye bags when Jay pulled up in his dark sedan.

I no longer asked if Sherlock could tag along, figuring Jay would let me know when it wasn't appropriate. Besides, we were going to a farm, and one that might be involved in an investigation. Sherlock would probably hang from Jay's bumper to get there if we didn't invite him into the cab.

Jay turned onto the main drive before he started talking. "I've put out an APB with a description of Carla. She's not local, and the only Carla Whitley I could find listed in Oregon is from a couple of hours up state. If she's still in Crystal Cove, though, I intend to find her."

I nudged a container of cinnamon buns toward Jay between the seats. I'd sent a couple home with Katie, never wanting to let Olivia's baking go to waste. Jay glanced down and smiled at the sight of them, but didn't dig in. Not while he was driving, but more importantly, not while he was so focused on a case.

"When I questioned him again, Dr. Gray mentioned a red-haired woman that had come into the morgue to identify her brother right after his death. Apparently, she had wanted an autopsy, and he had to explain to her three times that the cause of death was clear. She left without signing the papers to release the body to the funeral home. On Friday, he had finally gotten hold of the parents, and they said they would make sure the sister returned to deal with the paperwork that day."

"That's why Dr. Gray had made arrangements to have the body picked up by the funeral home Friday evening, and why he'd been unable to follow through on that?" Before he answered, another question occurred to me. "Can we get in touch with Carla through her parents? You said Dr. Gray has their number?"

Jay nodded. "Already tried. It rings and rings and there's no voicemail. If we haven't discovered anything about her current whereabouts by this afternoon, I'll have to make a call to the police upstate and ask them to stop in on the woman and/or her parents."

Jay's phone rang, and he clicked on the Bluetooth to answer it through the speakers of his car.

"What have you got," Aaron's voice said through the speakers.

"You said Shep Whitley's sister came into the station, claiming there had been foul play in her brother's death? What information do you have on that?"

"Just some scattered notes." We heard papers shuffling. "It wasn't worth filing a report about it, as the medical examiner had a clear cause of death on his initial report and it seemed like the woman's suspicions were only caused by shock and grief."

"What was the name of the sister? And her description?"

When Aaron confirmed it was Carla Whitley and that she had red curly hair, Jay explained all I had learned the night before.

Aaron cut him off before he could get the whole story out. "This Carla Whitley still thought there was something fishy about her brother's death, and was looking for another way to prove it? So she wanted the church members to try and raise him from the dead?" Aaron's voice was usually stoic, so the disbelief in it now surprised me.

"She went to the witches to try and connect with his spirit. We think Marigold talked her into trying to raise him from the dead. She went to the Harvest Festival for prayer first, though. We're headed to the Morty farm now to see if there church folks were somehow involved. All I can guess is that the church ladies for some reason redirected her to the witches, although I can't imagine why, since the two groups didn't exactly get along."

"Maybe that *is* why," I blurted, before I thought better of it.

Jay glanced away from the road to look at me while Aaron was silent.

"I mean, as nice of a festival the church put on, if this lady was so crazed—and Jay and I saw that she was—maybe the church ladies would have decided to unload the problem onto the witches instead?"

"Huh." Aaron said. And then after a few seconds he said it again. "Huh." A long pause followed while we all digested this possibility. "Well, let me know if you can confirm that theory out at the Morty farm. In the meantime, I'm going to drop in on Ms. Weathers and put some pressure on her to tell the truth."

I bit back my smile. Not because Marigold was in trouble with the local police. I still counted her as a friend, even after how she treated me, as now at least I understood why she'd been so secretive. If any of the other witches had discovered Shep's body on Friday night, they would have gone to her first, not the police. But I was the first on scene, and as far as she was concerned, I ruined her entire opportunity to try some of her magic in a life-and-death sense, and to make a good profit from it.

But what made me infinitely happy was that Aaron was the one putting the pressure on Marigold for some real answers and not Jay. If it was possible to come out of this on the other end without anyone who frequented the café becoming mortal enemies with another, that was my greatest hope.

Jay hung up as we arrived at the Morty farm. This time it didn't seem quite as easy as looking out over the field to find Hal Morty. With my suspicions of everyone involved heightened, it gave me the immediate sense that he was also avoiding the police.

But Jay headed straight for the young farmhand who was leading a horse by his reins toward a barn, and Sherlock and I followed quickly on his heels.

"Excuse me?" Jay called.

The boy turned around. He couldn't have been more than fifteen. "Is your dad around, Rand?"

Rand said, "Yup, in the barn. I'm headed there now."

Jay looked back at me, and in silent agreement, we followed Rand Morty toward the barn in the distance.

It was a long walk, and so I picked Sherlock up partway through. Any normal cat probably wouldn't tire so easily, but with Sherlock's short legs, he had trouble keeping up whenever we picked up our pace.

As soon as he was in my arms, he started purring, and by the time we reached the barn, he was in an all-out sleep.

That should have told me something. With his magical abilities and insight, if Sherlock didn't think there was anything to stay awake for here, there likely wasn't.

Hal Morty was exactly where Rand said he'd be. He was raking out a stall when we interrupted him, but he immediately leaned the rake against a side wall, ready for a break. Rand led the horse to another stall and by the time we'd all said hello to his dad, he grabbed the rake and took over where his dad left off.

"Looks like you're here on official business again," Hal said, looking between us. "Still that same case?"

Jay nodded. "We're looking for a person of interest in the case. Someone I saw at your Harvest Festival Friday night."

Hal pulled back in surprise. "He was here at the festival?"

"She," Jay corrected. "I believe she was from out of town. A lady with curly red hair named Carla?" Jay watched Hal carefully for recognition.

A second later a line appeared between his eyebrows. "Ahh, yeah, I remember her. She wanted some prayer. I think Edith and Mabel got a group of women together to help."

Jay nodded, making a note. "And did you see a man with her at all?"

He shook his head. "Nope, she was alone."

Jay made another note. "And have you seen this woman since?"

Hal shook his head and my heart sank. But then he said, "You should stop by the house, though. Talk to Mary. She's been nattering on about some upset with the local biddies." He let out a low chuckle. "Sorry, can't say I always listen to every word my wife says."

Jay chuckled along with him. "So you didn't see a bald man with a goatee? We saw him in the parking lot of the Harvest Festival."

Again, Hal seemed genuinely surprised at this. "Can't say I saw anyone of that description. Then again, I was running the hayrides. You might ask Mary about that one, too."

"All right. Will do. If you do hear from this woman, or a man of that description, would you let me know right away?"

"Sure thing, Jay." Hal wiped a dirty weathered hand on his jeans and then held it out for a shake.

Unfortunately, the farm house where we'd find Mary was in the opposite direction from where we'd parked. We hiked across the acres of grassy farmland as Sherlock snored quietly in my arms.

"Must be nice," I murmured down toward him.

When we arrived at the farmhouse, Mary answered the door, mid-conversation with someone on the phone. She was a stout woman probably in her mid forties, with broad shoulders that told me she probably did her share of farm work. She held up a finger toward us, but then said into the receiver, "Listen, Mabel, I've got some company. Can I call you right back?"

After hanging up and putting her phone down inside, she returned to open the door wide for us. "Detective? To what do I owe this pleasure?"

It was a good sign that Hal hadn't called to warn his wife of our presence. Jay had taught me that. When you arrived to interview someone and they seemed to already know too much information about why you were there, that could be an immediate red flag.

"This is my friend, Tabitha. She's helping me with a case and we're looking for someone who was at the Harvest Festival Friday night. A lady from out of town? Red curly hair?"

Right away, Mary nodded with recognition. "Funny, Mabel and I were just talking about her. Her name's Carla…Whitley, I think?" Mary glanced down at Sherlock, but didn't mention him. I was betting she was more used to tough farm cats than cuddly intuitive ones.

Jay nodded. "And what were you discussing?"

"Well, she was some upset Friday night. She showed up here wanting us to pray for her dead brother. She wanted the ladies to try to talk to his spirit." Mary let out a long sigh under her breath. "I mean, we believe in holy miracles, but that sort of thing sounds more like witchcraft."

It all lined up with what we'd learned so far.

"And so did you pray for her, or did you send her off to talk to the local witches?" Jay asked.

"Well, I had to tend to the carnival games. I was overseeing that whole area for the evening, so I really wasn't part of the whole ordeal, but I don't suppose Edith would have let her leave without at least praying for her."

"And do you know if Edith then directed her to see the witches?"

Mary looked back in the direction where the festival had been. "I'm afraid I couldn't say." By the way she avoided our eyes, I wasn't sure I believed this, but we could certainly ask Mabel and Edith for their side of things if Mary didn't want to own up to it.

"And have you seen this lady since Friday night?" Jay asked.

"Not me, no," Mary said. "But she's been staying with Edith."

My eyes darted to Jay, who was already writing. "Edith Jenkins?"

Mary nodded. "That's right. Well, you met her, too, Detective Jameson. That was the same woman who was hit by a car!"

Jay wrote furiously with all of these details. "I'm afraid I didn't meet her. By the time I got here, Detective Ross had already sent her off in an ambulance."

"Oh, right." Mary nodded down at the floor, like this made sense. "Anyway, the woman—Carla—was still some shaken up when Edith went to see her in the hospital the next day. Edith took her home for the night, but now the lady hasn't wanted to leave. She's been weeping all day every day, and none of us know who to call for her or what to do to help."

Jay nodded as he closed his notepad. "Don't you worry about it, Mary. I'll get over to Ms. Jenkins' house and handle this."

Mary inclined her head and took one of his hands in both of hers. "Thank you, Detective."

We reached the car and let out a collective breath—me, Jay, and Sherlock.

"We found her," Jay said. "Maybe we can tie up this case today, after all."

Chapter Twenty-one

Fifteen minutes later, solving the case today didn't look as promising. Edith answered the door looking much more haggard than when I'd seen her at the Harvest Festival.

"Hi, Edith," Jay said. "We understand you've had a houseguest for the last few days. A woman named Carla Whitley?"

Sherlock had followed us from the car, and Edith didn't notice as he nosed past her ankles into the house.

She harrumphed loudly before answering. "That's right."

I widened my eyes, surprised at her rudeness.

"The woman has needed a shoulder to cry on. Finally, I think she's dried herself out of her tears. She left for a short time. I suggested she go get some fresh air."

"Where did she go?" Jay and I asked at the same time. "Do you know if she left town?" Jay added.

"I don't think so. She still has a few things here in my spare room, but when she comes back I think it's time to broach the subject of her heading home."

"It was nice of you to take her in," I said, as Jay was making notes. I had the sense he could use a moment to get over his frustration about this. "I hear you invited her to stay because she sustained some injuries from being hit by a car Friday night. Do you think she's well enough to drive home now?"

Edith heaved out a sigh. "Whether she is or whether she isn't, I'm afraid her needs are more than one person alone can handle. I thought some of the other local ladies would lend a hand with her, but apparently not so."

"Can you tell me about what, exactly, happened with Carla on Friday evening?" Jay asked. "I understand she came to you wanting prayer?"

Edith nodded. "She was some upset about her brother's passing. Sometimes grief makes us believe some far-fetched ideas. When my husband Henry passed, I woke up each day for a month and cooked bacon and eggs, somehow believing that if I had his favorite breakfast ready, he might be there with me to eat it."

I dipped my head, feeling compassion, but also wanting to get her back onto the topic of Carla. "And Carla believed some far-fetched ideas as well?"

Edith offered a sad smile and nodded. "Poor thing thought that with enough prayer, her brother would come back to her and tell her what really happened to him."

"What did she think happened to him?" I blurted, and then quickly checked in with Jay to make sure I wasn't over-stepping, but his gaze was set on Edith and he didn't seem bothered by my question.

Edith sighed again. "She said it was too coincidental, that her brother Shep died so close to where her other brother lives. She was terribly afraid that her brother may have been so full of hate, he'd done something."

My heart stuttered and I looked to Jay, the word "Murder" automatically reverberating through my mind.

Jay wasn't nearly as rattled by this information. "Did Carla bring her deceased brother to you for prayer?"

It was a bold question. I looked back to Edith, but her head was tilted, like she didn't understand.

Jay clarified. "Did she have his body along with her? Perhaps in her vehicle?"

Edith's eyes widened. "Why, no, I don't think so. Although, come to think of it, she did try to steer us back toward the parking lot to pray. Because she was so distraught, I thought it better to keep her within the lit area of the festivities."

"And after you prayed for her, did you direct her to visit the local witches?" Jay's words were soft. I was glad he was being gentle with Edith, as I had the sense she had only been trying to do what was right.

Edith nodded. "Not in as many words, but she could have certainly construed it that way. She kept wanting us to pray and try to connect with her brother's spirit. I told her that sounded more like a job for the local witches." Edith's jaw tensed as she said this.

"And did you tell Carla where she could find the local witches on Friday night?"

I saw a glint in Edith's eye before she bowed her head and nodded.

The feud between the witches and the church was no longer our biggest concern, though. We were getting a much clearer picture of what had happened Friday night.

One thing still didn't make sense to me, though. "When did she get hit by the car? Did she return to the Harvest Festival later that night?"

Edith nodded. "She was even more out of her mind the second time she showed up. She grabbed my arms and said something about her boyfriend's car, the police, and again about her brother, Shep. I couldn't make heads or tales of her words, and next thing I knew, she was running for the parking lot, shouting "Erik!" and a car came out of nowhere and knocked her up onto the hood and then onto the ground. Then the car was gone in a flash, and we called 911."

Poor Edith looked like she was reliving the whole experience in front of us.

Jay pulled out a business card. "You've been more than helpful, Edith. Can you please call me the moment Carla returns? I really need to speak to her, and I'll find a way to take the burden off of you."

I had the sense Jay wasn't talking about bringing Carla back to his own home. He was more likely considering locking her up in a cell at the local jail. But now my heart hurt for everyone involved, because what if Carla was right, and there had been foul play in her brother's death? She may not have gone about trying to find the facts of the matter in the right way, but if the police wouldn't listen, I almost couldn't blame her, and I certainly couldn't deny I understood her need to know the truth.

Jay and I left Edith's front stoop and I was surprised to see Sherlock waiting at the car. He could be stealthy when he wanted to be.

"Where do we look next?" I asked as we all got in.

"Not sure." Jay started the car. "But Aaron has the whole police force on it. Let's hope he turns something up."

Chapter Twenty-two

No sooner had we pulled into the police station than Jay's radio crackled to life with Aaron's voice on the other end, telling Jay to go to a different channel.

"Ms. Weathers has confirmed a lot of what we'd suspected, but more importantly, we've turned up someone of a similar description to Carla Whitley near the local hospital. What's your ten-twenty?" he asked. "You near enough you could stop by and see if it's her? I told Officer Dante to stand down and keep her in sight for now."

Jay clicked on his radio and put his car into gear. "Just around the corner. I'm on my way."

We found her? The voice was so clear, for a split second I thought Jay had asked it, and I answered him before I realized it was Sherlock's inner voice.

"It sounds like we did."

Jay looked at me strangely, which clued me into how I was having a conversation with my cat again. This time, in front of him.

To cover, I quickly added, "I wonder if she's lurking around the morgue, trying to get back in to see her brother."

"That was my first thought, too."

He connected with Officer Dante to find out Carla's exact location, which was behind a tree, twenty feet away from the morgue entrance, watching the doors.

After Jay disconnected with Officer Dante, he glanced my way as he pulled into the hospital parking lot. "I have an idea." He clicked on his Bluetooth and instructed it to call Dr. Gray.

We couldn't see the morgue entrance from here, nor could we see Carla, but I recognized Officer Dante, sitting in plain clothes on a bench facing the hospital, pretending to read a newspaper. While Jay's phone rang, I asked, "What are you thinking?" But he didn't have time to answer me before Dr. Gray picked up.

"Listen, it's Detective Jameson here. I'm going to need your help with something. Can you leave the morgue through the doors into the hospital and lock them behind you? Leave the ones to the outside ramp open."

"I'm the only one here," Dr. Gray said. "I can't leave it unattended."

That hadn't seemed to have stopped him on Friday night.

"I'm monitoring the area from the outside. I'll be certain to keep a close eye. Is Shep

Whitley the only body you have on site at the moment?"

"Yes…" he drew out the word as though he was considering his instructions from the local police. "Our forensic examiner left for the lab a few minutes ago. I still haven't put Mr. Whitley back into the cooler."

"Actually, that's perfect," Jay said. "I need you to clear the place for a few minutes. Keep your phone on and I'll tell you when you can return." Jay hung up on him, which I suspected was one of his detective tactics to not allow for argument.

Then he turned to me. "Now it's your turn. Can you do something for me?"

I straightened in my seat. "Of course." No matter what it was, I could not envision myself refusing him. Especially when Sherlock meowed from the backseat, as though he was trying to volunteer for the part.

Jay pointed. "I want you to go into the morgue through the outside doors. Come out a few seconds later with your phone to your ear, telling some imaginary person on the other end that you stopped at the morgue but there's no one there to help you. The place was unattended. Say it loud enough that Carla might hear you."

My palms started to sweat, but I pulled out my phone, regardless. This was something I could help with. Besides, what he suggested made a lot of sense.

"You want to see if she tries to steal the body again?" I asked.

He scanned the surrounding area. "Maybe not *steal* it in broad daylight, but if I can catch her in the act of at least tampering, I'd have enough reason to bring her in and pressure her with some specific questions."

"But what if she had a good reason to want to try and find out what really happened to her brother? What if she's right about his death involving foul play?"

Jay's eyes flicked back and forth over mine, and I could see his own compassion warring with his need to uphold the law. "Yes, but what if she's not?"

I didn't believe that, but I guessed that would be for her to explain to a judge. Without any more direction, I opened the car door to make good use of the few minutes Dr. Gray may or may not have given us. I leaned into the car one last time before heading for the morgue. "What if Dr. Gray is still inside?"

Jay sighed. "Then you'll have to explain our purpose to him. Use your charm."

He winked at me and I felt the sea glass around my neck warm. I didn't have a lot of confidence that I could be charming on my own, but hopefully my sea glass would help to give me the words.

Chapter Twenty-three

THE MORGUE WAS UNATTENDED. Dr. Gray had done exactly as Jay had asked, and left Shep's body on the metal table in the center of the room. He'd thrown a white sheet over him, for which I was thankful.

I held my breath, trying to avoid smelling the mix of formaldehyde and other chemicals that were all too familiar to me from the last several days, spent less than ten seconds within the actual morgue, and then headed back outside with my cell phone to my ear.

I could see Carla off to my right in my peripheral vision. She was near a tree, but didn't hide when she saw I was only a patron leaving the morgue.

"Yeah, this is the third time I've been to the morgue when no one has been here," I said, adding a little anger to make my voice louder. "I can't believe they leave the doors open with no one even there watching the place. There was even a body on the table, but don't worry, it wasn't grandpa. It was some younger guy." My sea glass became warmer and warmer as the words slid seamlessly off of my tongue.

I had just passed Carla when she skirted behind me and through the double doors toward the morgue. The doors had barely shut behind her when Jay appeared at my side, ready to follow her in. But I put a hand out to stop him.

"Let me," I said. "Just for a minute. I have an idea."

He studied me for a moment, but then nodded.

My sea glass continued to pulse with warmth as though it was a living, breathing thing as I moved back for the doors. My intention was not so much to catch Carla in the act, but rather to gather a little intel that the police may not be able to get.

I didn't attempt to be quiet as I moved back through the doors. I said, "I'm telling you, there's no one in there, Tammy," as if into my phone. "But if you insist, I'll go back in and leave a note."

I slid my phone into my purse, and when I pushed through the second set of doors into the morgue, Carla stood between me and her brother's body, as though protecting him from any intruders. The sheet had been removed from his head, and I tried to keep my gaze away from his sunken face.

"Oh. Hi," I said, as if surprised. "Do you work here?"

Carla shook her head. Her red hair was much messier than it had been Friday night, and that had been a shock of a mess. I wondered if she'd even brushed it since then.

"Well, do you know where Dr. Gray is? I need to talk to him about my grandfather." I took in a big breath and then tried to cover the shock of the scents hitting my nose, by pulling out a tissue and wiping away imaginary tears.

Carla shook her head, but still looked like a deer in the headlights, like she thought I'd caught her. That wasn't going to work to help her relax any and open up to me.

I let out a loud harrumph. "I sure wish there was another morgue in town I could deal with. My whole family would feel better if we knew for sure it was his heart, but it seems like Dr. Gray can't tell us anything. Don't you wish you could take care of things yourself sometimes? Grandpa deserves better than this!"

The rant was exactly what Carla needed. Her eyes sparkled with renewed life as I said the words that she must have felt. She nodded slowly. "I was trying. To take care of him myself. My brother," she added, clearly out of sorts about the whole thing. Then she murmured something I could barely hear, but it sounded like, "If only I could find that witch again."

"What happened to him?" I motioned to Shep's face, without looking directly at it. "He's very young."

She nodded. "Dr. Gray says he ate some poisoned mushrooms while he was hiking. He doesn't even like mushrooms." She shook her head and looked at the floor.

"If you don't think it was the mushrooms, what do you think really happened?" My intense curiosity made it difficult to keep the soft tone to my voice, but I forced myself to slow down as much as I could.

"I don't have any proof, but it's all too coincidental—him hiking right near Bart's house. The mushrooms…" She shook her head again. "I just need to know."

"You do." I nodded in solidarity. "And your brother deserves better than being laid to rest here, without the whole truth." I pulled out an old receipt from my purse and a pen. I jotted down my name and my number and then put the slip down on a side metal table. When I turned back around, Carla was staring at her brother's face in deep thought. I added, "If Dr. Gray comes back, can you tell him to call me. I left my number." I pointed to the paper. "I only wish there was something else I could do to get my grandpa out of here sooner."

I shook my head and left through the morgue doors.

Carla hadn't told me anything really new, but the intense warmth of my sea glass indicated I'd said the right words, the ones that would egg her on. When I returned to Jay outside, I told him, "Why don't you give her two more minutes?"

He opened his mouth, but then closed it again. Then he opened it again. "I can't leave her in there with a body that's in the midst of an autopsy. We can't take the chance of her tampering with it."

Shoot. That made sense. I stepped out of his way.

I didn't think this would have given Carla anywhere near enough time to incriminate herself in any way, but when Jay moved stealthily through the outside doors, I held the door behind him so it wouldn't clack shut.

That gave me the opportunity to see that it actually had been enough time.

Because Carla was in the middle of the hallway, wheeling her dead brother on the gurney toward the outside world, covered again with the white sheet.

Chapter Twenty-four

An hour later, Jay had pacified Dr. Gray about the moved body and brought Carla back to the police station. I was more than a little surprised when he suggested, "Can you come into the interrogation room with me?" even though Aaron was in the office, and would probably have been a better choice.

"I guess…" I hedged.

"You seemed to know what to say to Carla back there at the morgue. If you get a sense from her where we should focus to get to the truth, I want you to feel free to jump in on the conversation."

I nodded, stroking Sherlock. Thankfully, no one batted an eye any longer when I brought my cat with me into the police station. They probably thought he was an emotional support therapy animal. In some ways, maybe he was.

When we entered the interrogation room, Carla sat on one side of an empty table, with only a box of tissues in the center. There were two empty chairs across from her, which Jay and I took. There wasn't any glass, like those one-sided windows you always saw in interrogation rooms on TV. In fact, I didn't see any recording equipment at all.

But then I noticed a tiny nodule in the top corner of the room, and figured that must capture the words and actions of anyone being interrogated in here. The thought of being watched made me feel immediately on edge. It must have been making Carla feel the same way, or maybe she was showing her anxiety, because her movements all looked twitchy, almost like she was detoxing from drugs.

"Good afternoon, Ms. Whitley," Jay said as we sat. It seemed a strange formality, considering he had brought her here less than half an hour ago. He had not handcuffed her, and in fact, he had not even placed her under arrest. She also had not resisted when he'd told her he needed to bring her down to the local police station for questioning. "Can you tell me how long you've been staying in Crystal Cove?"

She nodded. Her eyes looked worried, but I sensed she was being completely forthright when she said, "Since Friday."

"Friday, October 31st?" Jay confirmed, to which she nodded her agreement. "And can you tell me the purpose for your visit?"

Her twitches became stronger, almost erratic. "I had to… Shep…" she shook her head, but Jay and I both waited her out as she tried to come up with the words. "My brother, he died, and… he had to…I had to…they needed me to sign off…"

When time stretched on and it didn't seem like she was going to be able to get the words out, Jay filled in the rest of her sentence for her. "Were you here to sign off on releasing your brother's body from the morgue?" His voice was gentler than I'd ever heard it, and it was probably this, more than anything else that made me hope he wouldn't have to actually arrest this woman for her transgressions. It was clear to me that Carla Whitley was simply a sister in mourning who had made some bad choices due to her grief.

Carla nodded, looking at her lap.

Jay had his notepad on the table and made a note before asking his next question. "And was it Dr. Gray who asked you to come into town to do this paperwork?"

"I—I don't know. I think so." When Jay left her words hanging, she eventually added more. "My parents are elderly, in no shape to travel, and they took his calls. They were trying to get my other brother to go and identify Shep last Monday, but Bart didn't want to. I drove down to do it myself on Tuesday, but Bart's refusal got me to thinking about how much he'd hated Shep. I identified Shep's body, as they wanted me to, but I wouldn't sign the release papers and instead came right here to the police station. Except no one would listen, so I went back home. I guess I hoped that if I refused to accept his body, it would force the police and everyone else to look more closely into his death."

The thirty-something woman with the elderly parents made me think momentarily of Katie. Although, even though I'd only recently met Katie, somehow I knew she would be able to take care of the details of a family member's death with much more stability.

Carla's jeans were dirty and loose and I suspected she'd been wearing the same pair every day since Friday. She pulled a tissue from the box on the table and blew her nose. "My parents insisted I come back to deal with the paperwork. They wouldn't listen to any of my suspicions either."

Jay noted this. "Did you come town alone?"

She shook her head. "When I had to come back a second time, my boyfriend Erik came with me."

"And so you arrived at the morgue at what time on Friday?" Jay asked.

She looked up, thinking. "Around eight or eight-thirty, I think. I had to wait for Erik to get off work."

Jay made a note of the boyfriend's name and asked for his last name as well. "So you went into the morgue at around eight-thirty. And did you speak to Dr. Gray?"

She shook her head. "There was no one in there except my poor brother, all alone." Her body shook like she was starting to cry again, but no tears streamed down her face. I suspected she'd long ago emptied her tear ducts.

"So what did you do?" Jay barely had the question out of his mouth when he held up a hand to stop her from answering. He checked his cell phone, which was buzzing, and then said, "I'm sorry. I have to take this." He angled his notepaper over to me and passed me his pen. "Tabby, can you continue?"

I was surprised, but then not as much when Jay stood and simply moved over near the door, murmuring quietly into his phone.

I concentrated on my own job. "What did you do, Ms. Whitley, when you found your brother in the morgue alone?"

A crease formed between her eyebrows. "I told Erik we had to take him back home. First no one would believe me that Shep's death wasn't an accident, and then they left him all alone there! No one seemed to care about him at all, no one except for me. I only wanted to get him out of this town, back to a place where he'd been loved and where his death meant something. Erik didn't want to at first, but I begged him and I was an awful mess, so eventually he helped."

I made a note of this, wondering at her describing herself as an awful mess then. "So you carried your brother, Shep Whitley, out of the morgue and put him where?"

She nodded. "Into the backseat of Erik's car."

"And where did you go, once you had him in the car?"

A crease formed between her eyes as she recounted the details. "We were on our way out of town and there was this big church group. I made Erik stop so I could ask them if they'd pray for Shep, maybe help me get some guidance on what really happened to him." She shook her head. "But they only wanted to pray for me and my grief. Then one of the old ladies there said what I was asking for sounded like a job for the local witches. She sent me to an address where they would all be that night and told me not to hesitate to interrupt their fundraiser to ask for their help."

"And that's what you did?" I could imagine the church biddies thinking this crazed woman would surely put a kink in the witches' Fright Night. I could also understand why they hadn't been in any hurry to tell Jay about this.

Carla nodded. "When we got there, the one witch with purple hair said it might be difficult to connect with Shep, and she'd have to have calm and silence. She told me we'd have to wait until their fundraiser was over. I tried to convince her to try earlier, but then she started making excuses, like that she'd never actually connected through a third party, and usually she needed to be near the body of the person. She seemed surprised when I told her I had his body right in the car. Then she told me if I went by a local rosemary farm she knew of and quietly picked some rosemary, that would help enhance his spirit so she'd be able to hear him better. It still kind of sounded like an excuse, but I did what she said."

Jay interrupted us momentarily, coming over to leave me a couple of sheets of paper and take his notepad over to where he was having his quiet conversation. He pulled out another pen from his breast pocket as he asked, "So the fungus was only a misdirect?"

I wanted to listen in on what he was saying, but I also wanted to get back to Carla's story, as it seemed she had no problem being completely honest and forthright, especially when it was only me asking the questions. "And so you picked some rosemary and returned to the fundraiser?"

"Back to the purple-haired witch." Carla nodded with eyes that looked wide and trusting and somehow innocent. "But then she said we were too early. I begged her to come to Erik's car and at least try. Then she went and turned out the lights of their mansion so no one would see, and told me to put Shep into a bathtub. Erik didn't want to help, especially when the witch told us we had to come back at midnight. But then as Erik was saying he was getting Shep and getting out of there, the purple-haired witch said she would even try to raise Shep back up to life again! It sounded like she could really do it, too, so how could I refuse?"

"And this purple-haired witch, do you know her name?" She shook her head, so I jumped in right away with my next question. "Were any other witches involved, to your knowledge?" Another head shake. "Did she charge you any money for this promised miracle?"

She nibbled her lip and her face flushed, like she was embarrassed about this. Eventually she nodded. I was about to ask how much, but Jay's words were a little louder in the silence.

"Paraquat? How do you spell that?" As Jay listened and wrote on his notepaper, Carla stood from her place at the table, tilting her head at Jay with widened eyes.

"What happened with Paraquat?"

Whatever Jay was murmuring, he stopped mid sentence when Carla stepped closer toward him.

He narrowed his eyes toward Carla, cupped a hand over the mouthpiece of his phone and asked, "Do you know the substance Paraquat?"

She nodded fervently. "My brother Bart's a landscaper and he uses that herbicide for everything. He orders it from overseas, because apparently that's the only way to get it without the ugly blue color."

Jay's eyes stayed on Carla as he took one deep breath, then another.

Then he took his hand from the phone mouthpiece and said, "Thank you for getting back to me so quickly, Dr. Gray. I think you're right. I think this information is very significant."

Chapter Twenty-five

WHEN JAY SAT ACROSS the table from Carla again, and encouraged her to sit back down as well, everything about him looked calm. It was the sea glass burning against my skin that tipped me off that something very big had changed in the last five minutes.

He didn't return to my line of questioning, even though I had all but gotten to the part where she left her brother's body in a haunted house and paid a witch to try to magically raise him from the dead.

The fungus was a misdirection. Did that mean Carla was right about this death involving foul play? Did her brother Bart poison Shep?

"Tell me about this other brother of yours," Jay said, casually, but I knew him well enough to hear the seriousness behind the words. "You said his name was Bart? Where does Bart live?"

Carla drew a deep breath. "Just a few miles inland from here. That's why my parents thought it would be much easier for him to come and identify...Shep." I could tell Carla also sensed something had changed, and now it seemed as though her suspicions were keeping her emotions in check, or at the very least, in the background.

"And how was the relationship between Bart and Shep? Was there brotherly love there?"

She had already told us this, but that had been before the police had really been listening to Carla's theory. My mind flashed back to my snippets of dreams.

"Did he do it? Did he kill Shep?" Her question seemed to suck all the air out of her, and maybe even out of the entire room. Even though she was the first to suspect her brother of murder, it seemed she hadn't truly believed it until this moment.

Jay's voice dropped to that gentle tone. "Ms. Whitley, can I get you to answer the question, please?"

Carla opened her hands on the table in front of her, stared into them, and shook her head. "Bart hated Shep. Shep was going to get my parents' inheritance, because he was a year and a half older than Bart." She swallowed hard and looked up at Jay. "Do you really think Bart did this?"

"I can't say for sure." Even though Jay said the words, I could sense the falseness in them. He knew it was true. "Do *you* think it's possible, Ms. Whitley?"

She let out a humorless harrumph. "It's more than possible. The problem is, if Bart did this, you'll never catch him." Carla sounded one hundred percent assured in that. "He's too smart. Too savvy."

I might have believed her. But my sea glass burned against my collarbone, and I knew if anyone could get to the truth and serve justice, it was Detective Jay Jameson.

Chapter Twenty-six

Carla didn't mind being sequestered in the interrogation room while Jay and I discussed the case with Aaron in a private office down the hall. In fact, I think she preferred it. She wanted Jay to get to the bottom of what happened to her brother Shep more than anything else, and was happy to stick around in case she could help.

"What have we got?" Aaron asked as Jay and I entered the office and sat. "A new development I should know about?"

"You could say that." Jay turned his mess of notes toward the senior detective, but Aaron kept his eyes on Jay as he rattled off details. "It looks to me like first degree murder. The younger brother, a local from a few miles inland, did it. Now we have to prove it."

Aaron immediately grabbed at the pile of notes and read, his brow furrowed like he was angry at them. "It can't be," he said, under his breath, and in that second, in the angry defensiveness that oozed through Aaron's every pore, I knew he had been the detective who had dismissed Carla's concerns over her brother's death.

Jay kept his gaze from Aaron as he explained the rest of the details. The motive of the inheritance. The means of having the same herbicide that had been used as the murder weapon, hidden by some poisonous mushrooms.

"We haven't spoken to Bart yet, and because Shep Whitley was found up in the woods, it'll be hard to place Bart at the scene," Jay went on. "The sister, Carla, expects her brother Bart to be able to talk his way out of anything."

Aaron looked up and met Jay's eye, his jaw set with determination. "What we really need to tie this thing up is a confession."

"Carla says we'll never get it." Even though I had faith in my detective friends, Jay didn't feel as assured. "Maybe if you and I worked him over together…" Jay suggested.

Aaron clicked on his computer and looked up Bart Whitley's address. He pursed his lips. "It's outside our jurisdiction."

"But the murder was within our boundaries," Jay argued, clearly eager to head out the door, regardless of rules.

Aaron shook his head. "Shep wasn't local, and even though he died within our jurisdiction, with this brother of his living outside of the area, it's really a job for the state police."

"It's ten miles out, Thom!"

Aaron raised his eyebrows, like he was waiting for Jay to make his point. When Jay didn't immediately speak, Aaron stood and headed for the door.

Jay followed him down the hallway. "By the time the state police get down here… And the paperwork that'll take…" Jay held his hands out and shook them, like what he really wanted to do was shake his superior by the shoulders to make him see reason.

But then an idea came to me. I ran to catch them in the hallway, just as Aaron reached for the door of the interrogation room where Carla was situated. "Wait!" I interrupted them, immediately so convinced of my idea, I had to share it. They both looked over at me. "What if you sent Carla in wearing a wire?"

Chapter Twenty-seven

I COULD IMMEDIATELY TELL that Jay and Aaron were both uncomfortable with such an outside-the-lines maneuver, but I pled with them. "Carla would do anything to bring justice for what happened to Shep." I gave Aaron By-the-Books Thom a long look, as I suspected he would be the more difficult to convince. "Let's at least tell her the risks and see if she's willing."

The door swung out of Aaron's hand and Carla stood on the other side. "Of course I'm willing! Anything you need. Just tell me what to say."

Jay turned and murmured to me. "I'm not sure this is a good idea, Tabby." Worry filled his eyes. "The woman is clearly in distress."

My sea glass warmed, assuring me we were on the right track. "Jay, I think it's our only option."

Aaron nodded, surprising me. "Be truthful. Tell him you've talked to the police. Tell him you were brought in for questioning. Tell him we know Shep wasn't killed by a wild mushroom, but by an herbicide, the same herbicide he uses for his business."

Between Aaron being on board with the idea and Carla's willingness to take the risk, Jay's concerns seemed to melt away, and he joined in the planning.

Carla's biggest argument was that her brother Bart would see right through her, but Jay told her, "The only thing you have to keep quiet about is the fact that you're wearing a wire."

She looked between the three of us, but her gaze landed on me when she asked, "And you'll be nearby if I need you?"

I didn't check with Aaron or Jay, for fear that they might leave me behind. "Absolutely," I told her. My sea glass warmed again, as if in response.

As Aaron led the charge in preparing, I had the feeling he was only considering this ploy because he knew Jay was right about involving the state police. Not only that, I suspected he felt responsible for dismissing Carla's concerns in the first place.

"Do you have a car in town?" Aaron asked Carla. "It would look less conspicuous if you arrived in your own vehicle."

She shook her head. "Erik drove me here Friday, and he got so panicked to get out of town after the police showed up at the haunted house, he ended up hitting me with his car. I know he must feel guilty. I've been calling him ever since, and he won't call me back."

This woman had been through a lot. And now she was stranded in Crystal Cove because her boyfriend had almost run her over and then left her stranded on the side of the road? Some boyfriend. Jay and Aaron looked at each other, and I wondered if they were thinking they'd still try to bring charges on this Erik guy for the hit-and-run when this was all over.

We took Aaron's car. He usually preferred to be behind the wheel. Even though he wasn't too thrilled with me bringing Sherlock along in the back seat, he didn't argue, especially when Sherlock climbed into Carla's lap beside me and calmed her down with his purring.

Back at the station, Aaron had brought up Bart's property on Google Earth and had found a place for us to park out of sight. Unfortunately, there wasn't much of a shoulder in the area of the road where Bart lived, and the houses were acres apart, but Aaron eventually found a pullout with a stack of mailboxes where we could set up base a quarter of a mile down the road.

By the time we made it to the plot with the mailboxes, Jay had a laptop open on the middle console. They had attached the wire receiver to Carla's bra strap back at the station, and now he tested it to be sure it had a good connection.

"You're good to go, anytime you're ready," Jay told her gently.

I grasped her hand. "You can do this."

She met my eyes for a long moment, then reached for the door handle.

When she moved out of sight around the corner, the only thing that kept my racing pulse in check was the steady sound of her footsteps on gravel through the laptop.

I was pleased at the clarity of their connection with her. We should be able to hear every sound, even if Bart whispered.

Less than a minute later, Carla knocked on Bart's door. After a long wait, she knocked again. Finally, we heard a door open and a gruff voice ask, "What do you want?"

There was no brotherly love for Carla, it seemed, either.

"I have to talk to you."

A swishing sound and then a door shut. Carla, as scared as she was, had pushed her way inside. Go, Carla!

"What? Is this about Shep again?" His voice was loud and clear now that they were both inside his house. He didn't suspect he was being listened to, that much was obvious.

"Yes, it's about Shep! Did you know the cops brought me into the police station for questioning?"

"What are the cops questioning *you* about?" Now he sounded leery, like he knew why.

"They're talking about *murder*, Bart. They say Shep wasn't eating some mushroom in the woods that killed him. They say it was an herbicide!"

"Huh," Bart said, sounded less bothered than I would have expected. Even more so, when he added. "So what?"

"So *what?* It was the same kind of herbicide you use! I recognized the name Paraquat right away, and—"

"Did you tell them I use Paraquat?" His voice was suddenly sharp and angry.

"Well, I, uh… I didn't know… I wouldn't have…"

Shoot. Maybe Carla wasn't up for this task after all. Her brother sounded like he might be violent.

At that thought, I shook my head at myself. The man had committed murder, and of his own brother. Of course he was violent! And *I'd* suggested this.

Without asking permission, I reached for the door handle.

But then Bart let out a loud laugh. "Who cares! Every landscaper worth his salt uses Paraquat. They'll never know it was me."

Carla's trembling voice asked, "It was… you?"

This laugh from Bart sounded less humor-filled. "All the rest of you care about is Shep, Shep, Shep. Maybe now that I got rid of him, Mom and Dad will see it's not worth ignoring me. It's in their best interest to give me what's mine and treat me with some respect."

This was all the confession Aaron and Jay needed. My hand was still resting on the door handle, but I hadn't made a move to get out until now, when both of them made swift moves to put the laptop aside and get out of the car.

"Respect?!" Carla sounded suddenly hysterical. "You killed your own brother and you want respect? The police are going to find you, you know. They already know about your special odorless colorless brand of Paraquat—"

"What?" he snapped. "They wouldn't know that unless you had told them."

Carla let out a sudden shriek, like she'd been pushed or hit.

I was torn between hearing the rest and going with Jay and Aaron to rescue her. Even though I wasn't sure what I'd be able to do to help, I had promised her I would be there for her if she needed me.

A second later, I was out of the car, along with Sherlock, and we ran to catch up to the two detectives.

Chapter Twenty-eight

THANKFULLY, BART HAD A sliding glass door off of his living room. That gave Jay and Aaron a chance to glimpse Carla and Bart as they moved from room to room. The three of us hid behind a bush off the back deck. The yard was sloped and behind us, on the only flat patch, was a wooden shed.

"He's got her wrists secured, but her feet are free," Jay observed. "It looks as though she's been struck on the cheek."

"He doesn't look armed," Aaron put in.

"I'm guessing he left the front door unlocked." Jay pulled a walkie talkie from his hip and passed it to me. "If you see him grab a weapon and head our way, give us a heads up."

Aaron frowned at Jay, then looked away, clearly fighting the urge to argue about involving me. But it was too late for that.

I nodded, suddenly terrified that I'd miss something crucial. But before I could express or even think through my concern, Aaron and Jay retreated around the house toward the front door.

A few seconds later, the walkie in my hand crackled to life. "Tabby?" came Jay's whisper. "How does it look? Is he still in the back hallway?"

I shook my head before depressing the button and saying, "I can't see either of them now. Where did they go?"

I'd barely gotten my rhetorical question out when a fleck of movement caught my eye inside. A second later, I realized the movement had been the edge of the front door opening, because Jay and Aaron were now inside.

They moved stealthily down the rear hallway, guns drawn, and checking around corners before they moved around each of them. I only caught short glimpses of them as they moved in and out of the living room, and I was so swept up in watching their movements, I almost missed the loud noise only ten feet behind me.

On instinct, I ducked around the shrub so I was now in full view of the living room, but hidden from the rest of the yard. I reached down and turned off the walkie talkie.

Seconds later, Bart's angry voice sounded on the other side of the bush, near the shed. "I'm going to fix you the same way I fixed Shep. Then Mom and Dad will have no choice but to stop ignoring me."

"They only ignore you because you're always so angry!" Carla's voice sounded frantic, but I couldn't see either of them on the other side of the bush. "They don't trust you, and now they're going to know that they can never trust you."

Bart laughed. "You think I don't know how to cover this up? They'll never know it was me, just like they'll never know I took care of Shep. I'll go back to their house, maybe even tonight. I'll put on a good act, shed a few tears for you and poor Shep. Then they'll finally know they shouldn't have cut me out of everything."

There was a thud, and then Carla let out a cry like the wind had been knocked out of her. He must have pushed her onto the ground. I started to make a move around the bush. I had to help her!

Before I could even take a step, Sherlock darted around my legs, around the bush, and out into the open near the shed, where I could no longer see him. But Bart and Carla most definitely could.

"I'll take care of that mangy thing at the same time," Bart said.

"No," Carla said, but not with much passion or volume. She sounded quietly determined, rather than frantic. Sherlock's presence alone could sometimes bring that kind of clarity and stability, but I had the sense this time it was because she knew we were all close. We were all looking for our opportunity to help her.

The shed door creaked open and Bart's voice sounded from farther away. "As you know, this stuff doesn't have much odor or taste, so it'll all be pretty painless, at least until it hits your intestines. But I'll have you well into the mountains by then. You'll be up there to honor your beloved brother in the only way you know how, by wandering up to where he took his last breath. Maybe I'll even put a few of those poisonous mushrooms in your mouth, like I did with Shep, so it looks like you were so grief-crazed you did yourself in the same way he did." Bart told his sister this casually, as though he was describing a meal he was preparing for her.

I glanced over my shoulder to see that Jay and Aaron were now all the way into the living room in plain view from my vantage point. It only took them a second to realize by my new position where Bart and Carla were now situated.

Aaron headed for the sliding glass door but only moved it an inch before he realized it was going to be too loud.

It was too late, though, because Bart heard it and said, "Who's out there?"

Aaron and Jay might have had time to get out of his vision, but I didn't. A second later, Bart charged around the bush, looked down at the walkie talkie in my hand, and then pulled me up by my jacket collar.

I was in big trouble.

Chapter Twenty-nine

"WHAT ARE YOU DOING on my property?" Bart aimed a gun toward me that none of us had seen. He was tall, like Carla, but outweighed her by at least double and had beefy muscles poking out of his shirt sleeves. "Get up!"

I stood from where I'd been crouching, and thought fast, the sea glass necklace burning around my neck. Why would I be here, on his property, with a walkie talkie in my hand. Why besides the real reason?

"I—my sister lives down the road," I said as it came to me. "I was playing hide-and-go-seek with my niece." I looked around and dropped my voice, my acting getting better and better by the second. "Have you seen her? She's supposed to stick to my sister's property, but she doesn't always follow the rules." I let my eyes stray to his gun and gave an exaggerated double-take. "Oh my gosh! Is that a real gun? Did you think I was breaking in or something? Oh, I'm so sorry! Listen, I'll just find my niece and be out of your way, all right?"

Bart narrowed his eyes at me. "What does your niece look like?"

I wondered if he expected me to describe Carla. I wasn't that dumb. Instead, I held up a hand near my shoulders, showing her height. "She's eleven." I was about to say she was a redhead like me, but the thought of Carla having red hair quickly made me change tack. "Blonde. Cute young thing, but she's a better hider than I ever was. That's why we always play with walkie talkies. In case we can't find her." I tilted the walkie back and forth in my hand, making clear I wasn't trying to hide it.

"We?" Bart asked, still suspicious.

I opened my mouth, and the answer came to me when Sherlock trotted around the bush, as if on cue. "Me and my cat. Sher…Sherman."

Unfortunately for me, Bart still found something in my story suspicious. He grabbed my arm roughly and said, "You're not going anywhere."

He started to pull me around the bush to where he'd left Carla, but Sherlock didn't like that idea.

I wouldn't expect such a short cat to be able to jump very high, but Sherlock never ceased to surprise me when I was in trouble. He launched himself high enough to get one set of claws into Bart's chest and the other into the arm that held the gun.

A gunshot rang out loud, hurting my ears, but it went straight into his sliding glass door, avoiding both me and Sherlock. Carla shrieked and flung herself from behind the bush to pound her tied fists on his back. With the distraction, I swung with all my strength toward his arm that held the gun. I hit his wrist with the walkie talkie and his hand involuntarily jerked open, releasing the weapon.

In the chaos of the moment, Jay and Aaron burst from around the rear of the house, guns drawn, and Aaron shouted, "Bart Whitley, drop the gun and get your hands in the air!"

Bart's gaze darted in all directions while his sister continued to shout incoherently and beat at his back: to me, now frozen in place with the walkie talkie in my hand, to the open shed door where a colorless liquid trickled out to seep into the ground, to my cat, still hanging from his arm where blood droplets were forming, and to the gun, fallen to the ground near his feet. Eventually he turned his attention back to the two detectives.

He raised his hands into the air.

Chapter Thirty

BY THE TIME AARON had cuffed Bart and led him back toward his sedan, Carla was in tears. At first, I figured the upset of having one of her brothers dead and the other one in custody was too much for her.

But then she looked up at Jay as he moved in closer to cut the zip tie holding her wrists together and she said, "I'm so sorry!" Her cheeks were streaked with tears.

"What are you sorry about?" Jay had her hands freed in mere seconds. "You helped us catch a murderer, and your own family member, no less."

She shook her head and motioned to the ground several feet behind her. "But I destroyed the evidence!" A white container lay on its side on the grass, the top off and the contents spilled out.

Jay almost laughed, but he suppressed it, putting her mind at rest before having a chuckle. "Thanks to you, we have the whole thing recorded. Even if Bart's guilt wasn't clear from the recording, our forensic scientists will be here soon to sample this grass, and I'll bet you dollars to donuts that your brother has more of this herbicide stashed right there in his shed."

I smiled at his phrasing. Leave it to a cop to make a point using the word donuts. I helped Carla to her feet. I still wondered if Jay was going to arrest her, too. She had stolen Shep's body from the morgue, after all. Then again, there were a lot of people who had broken, or at least bent the law in this case aside from

Carla: Her boyfriend, Erik, hitting her with his car and then leaving the scene; Marigold, in lying to the police about how Shep's body got into the haunted house and in unethically taking advantage of Carla; and even the other witches in town, who likely knew more about the situation with Shep than they had let on. Dr. Gray may not have been guilty of a crime, but he was certainly guilty of neglect of his duties at the morgue. I wondered if there would be consequences for any of them.

Back at the station, it seemed Jay and Aaron no longer needed my help. The end of a case was always bittersweet. In truth, I didn't want to be the one dealing with the mounds of paperwork that Jay was always complaining about, but I didn't like being pushed aside like yesterday's news, either.

As Jay walked me to the front door of the station, I asked, "Is anyone else going to get charged in all of this? What about Carla's boyfriend that hit her with his car?"

Jay nodded with a wry smile. "If he hadn't been speeding out of town on Friday, he might have gotten away with it. One of our officers pulled him over and quickly put it together that he'd been responsible for the hit and run. He's been in town the whole time, locked up and waiting for a hearing, unbeknownst to Carla."

I was glad to hear that, but considered how much easier it may have been to have solved this case if Jay had been the arresting officer and seen this bald man with the goatee with his own eyes.

"You should go home and get some rest," he told me as I left the station with Sherlock in my arms, ready to walk back to the marina. "And get this little guy a kitty treat or two." He scratched Sherlock on the back of the neck and Sherlock immediately started purring.

"You're sure?" I asked. I didn't really know what I was asking, because of course they didn't need my help to question a murderer and his sister and book the former into the local jail.

Jay said, "If it was up to me, Tabby, you'd be my partner on all my cases. But the captain just got in, and I have a feeling no matter how much I explain that we couldn't have solved the case without my cute redhead friend and her cat, I don't think he'd love the idea of the two of you sitting in on the booking."

I wanted to ask if it would have been different if Sherlock weren't with me. But I was too stuck on "cute redhead" to say anything at all.

The Heirloom Café was on my way back to the marina, so I stopped in, expecting to see Olivia behind the counter. Instead, I found Katie.

"I thought we were doing another training shift tomorrow afternoon," I said at the counter, surprised.

"Olivia needed to meet with an ex-boyfriend who was passing through town. I guess she couldn't get hold of you, so she called me to see if I'd fill in for a couple of hours."

An ex-boyfriend? That was curious. Every time I'd asked Olivia about her love life, she'd changed the subject on me. I was pretty sure she lived alone, but who was this mysterious ex, and why did she have to meet him on such short notice?

I glanced at my phone, only remembering now that I'd turned it off on our way to Bart Whitley's house. If I'd picked up, I may have heard more about her ex, but then I might not have been available to help solve a murder, so I figured I'd made the better choice.

"Can you make me a London Fog?" I asked Katie. Even though this was one of my favorite hot drinks, in truth, I was testing her. I hadn't taught her how to make one yet, and I wanted to see how she'd handle dealing with an unfamiliar drink on her own.

"You bet," she told me with a smile. "Have a seat and I'll bring it to you when it's ready. Oh, am I supposed to charge you?"

I pulled out some cash and passed it over. "If I'm not on shift? You bet."

She made my change and I sat at a nearby table, pretending to scroll on my phone while I watched her out of the corner of my eye. She had her phone in her hands, forehead creased as she read from her screen.

I was about to go and offer to make it myself while she watched to learn for next time, but before I could, she put down her phone, washed her hands, and reached for the container of earl gray at the back counter.

She brought me my drink less than two minutes later, and I took a sip. "Perfect," I told her, honestly.

She grinned. "It's been pretty slow. Anything else I should look up and learn while I have the time?"

I loved that she wasn't shy about areas she needed to learn. "Nothing I can think of, but it seems you've got a handle on things, even if someone does hit you up with a surprise order." I took another sip. "Your parents were okay to drive you into town on such short notice?"

"My mom was coming into town anyway. She planned to drop a resume off at the hospital."

I wondered if Jeff, the nurse who frequented The Heirloom Café with his girlfriend Jolie, would be able to pull any strings. I made a mental note to mention it the next time I saw him. "What's it like having older parents?" I asked her, my mind still half on Carla and her issue-ridden family.

She shrugged. "It's all I've ever known. But I can say that compared to my friends over the years, I've always had an easier time making my own rules. I think that's made me grow up fast."

I couldn't argue with that. Katie was smart and mature, and while she may have taken advantage of her parents' age once or twice over the years, I had the feeling it was always for good reason.

Before I left the café, I gave Katie my number and told her I could drive her home if her mom wasn't still in town.

Back at the boat, I heated up the rest of my soup for dinner and gave Sherlock a handful of cat treats on top of his usual kibble. He purred as he ate, and in between bites of soup, I flipped detective novels closed and placed them in their stacks off to the sides of the boat so it wasn't such an obstacle course to walk through. I also left them close enough that they might be of help for the next mystery we had to solve in Crystal Cove.

As I did that, I thought of how Sherlock had led me to the book Murder in New Orleans. I reread the back flap and recalled the story about the misdirection in what turned out to be a murder. At the time, I hadn't thought anything of it, as I hadn't thought Shep Whitley had been intentionally killed.

I looked over at my smart, intuitive cat. Aunt Lizzie had known exactly what she had been doing in taking him in.

Sherlock wriggled his nose, which made me look at the crystal in the center of his glasses. He meowed in my direction, as if telling me it was time to face up to my own magic.

I'd put my blue crystal beside my bed, but then quickly dismissed the dreams it had brought on. I shook my head at myself. How much more proof would I need to take these very real magical occurrences seriously? If I had paid attention, I could have helped Jay much more and much sooner. Even though Marigold hadn't followed through on her promise to contact Shep's spirit or raise him from the dead, in a way, the magic of Crystal Cove—the good magic we were known for—had helped Carla get to the truth.

It was time to learn more about my own magical abilities, those blue crystals, and how they had helped my Aunt Lizzie.

And I knew exactly where to start.

It was time to invite my mother for a visit.

The End.

* * *

If you'd like to read the bonus epilogue, where Tabby invites her mother to visit Crystal Cove, be sure to sign up for my

mailing list at
https://www.subscribepage.com/mysteryre
aders

And if you're ready for the next book
in the series, be sure to drop by
https://books2read.com/denisejaden where
you'll find links to all my e-books,
paperbacks, and hardcovers.

Turn the page for a couple of yummy
recipes…

Recipe – Tabitha's London Fog – With an Orange Twist!

Ingredients:

1 cup (250 mL) milk

1 large strip orange zest

1 Earl Grey tea bag

1/3 cup (80 mL) boiling water

1/4 tsp (1 mL) vanilla extract

1/2 tsp (2 mL) sugar (optional)

Orange zest for garnish

Preparation:

1. Heat milk over medium heat for about 3 minutes, or until steaming.

2. In a tall mug, combine orange strip, tea bag and boiling water; pour in half of the hot milk. Let steep for 5 minutes.

3. Froth the remaining hot milk with a battery-powered frother.

4. Remove orange strip and tea bag from your mug. Stir in vanilla and pour in remaining hot milk. Sweeten with sugar, if desired.

5. Garnish with finely grated orange zest and serve immediately.

6. Enjoy on its own or with the below coffee cake!

Tips:

Use a sharp vegetable peeler to peel strip of orange zest. Only peel the orange portion and avoid the white pith, which is bitter. For garnish, use a zester or a fine grater to shave the zest on top of the mug.

Recipe—Olivia's Banana Chocolate Walnut Cake

Tabby gets excited every time she sees overripe bananas on the café's counter. It means Olivia will make her delicious Banana Chocolate Walnut Cake soon!

Ingredients:

2 1/4 cups all-purpose flour

1 tsp baking soda

1/2 tsp salt

1 stick unsalted butter, softened, plus 2 tablespoons, melted and cooled

1 cup sugar, divided

2 large eggs

3 medium very ripe bananas, mashed

2/3 cup plain yogurt

1 tsp pure vanilla extract

3 1/2- to 4-ounces 70%-cacao bittersweet chocolate, coarsely chopped

1 cup walnuts - toasted, cooled, and coarsely chopped

1/2 tsp cinnamon

Preparation:

1. Preheat oven to 375°F with rack in middle. Grease a 9-inch square cake pan.

2. Combine flour, baking soda, and salt.

3. In a separate medium-size bowl, beat together softened butter (1 stick) and 3/4 cup sugar with an electric mixer at medium speed until pale and fluffy. Then beat in eggs 1 at a time until blended. Beat in bananas, yogurt, and vanilla (this mixture will look curdled).

4. With mixer at low speed, add flour mixture and mix until just incorporated. Do not overmix!

5. Toss together chocolate, nuts, cinnamon, melted butter, and remaining 1/4 cup sugar in a small bowl. Spread half of banana batter in cake pan and sprinkle with half of chocolate mixture. Spread remaining batter evenly over filling and sprinkle remaining chocolate mixture on top.

6. Bake until cake is golden and a wooden pick inserted in center of cake comes out clean, 35 to 40 minutes. Cool cake in pan on a rack 30 minutes and then turn out onto rack and cool completely.

7. Enjoy with your London Fog with a Twist!

Reviews Matter...

Honest reviews help bring new books to the attention of other readers. If you enjoyed this book, I would be grateful if you would take five minutes to write a couple of sentences about it. You can find all the books in this series to leave reviews at the following link. https://books2read.com/denisejaden

Thank you so much for your support. I couldn't do this without readers like you!

<u>**THE TABITHA CHASE DAYS of the Week Mysteries**</u>

Book 1 - Witchy Wednesday

Book 2 - Thrilling Thursday

Book 3 – Frightful Friday

Book 4 – Slippery Saturday

A Bookworm of a Suspect Mystery Anthology (Including Book 5 – Dead-end Weekend)

<u>**The Mallory Beck Cozy Culinary Capers:**</u>

Book 1 – Murder at Mile Marker 18

Book 2 – Murder at the Church Picnic

Book 3 – Murder at the Town Hall

Christmas Novella – Mystery of the Holiday Hustle

Book 4 – Murder in the Vineyard

Book 5 – Murder at the Montrose Mansion

Book 6 – Murder during the Antique Auction

Book 7 – Murder in the Secret Cold Case

Book 8 – Murder in New Orleans

Find all the Mallory Beck novels at Books2read.com/denisejaden

<u>Collaborative Works:</u>

Murder on the Boardwalk

Murder on Location

Saving Heart & Home

Nonfiction for Writers:

Writing with a Heavy Heart

Story Sparks

Fast Fiction

Acknowledgements

Thank you to my amazing team of advance readers, brainstormers, and supporters. I am so very thankful for every single one of you. Thank you to my amazing editor, Louise Bates, who makes my books infinitely better, my "Strange Facts Expert" Danielle, and my first (and most generous) reader, Monica. Thank you for joining me, along with Tabby and Sherlock, on this journey.
We're thrilled to have you along on this ride!

Denise Jaden is the author of the Mallory Beck Cozy Culinary Capers and the Tabitha Chase Days of the Week Mysteries. She has also written several critically-acclaimed young adult novels, as well as nonfiction books for writers, including the NaNoWriMo-popular guide Fast Fiction. In her spare time, Denise acts in TV and movies and dances with a Polynesian dance troupe. She lives just outside Vancouver, British Columbia, with her husband, son, and one very spoiled cat.

Sign up on Denise's website to receive bonus content (you'll find clues in every bonus epilogue!) as well as updates on her new Cozy Mystery Series.

www.denisejaden.com